# TECH IT TO RIDE

HEIDE GOODY

IAIN GRANT

# 1

Randolph was never daunted by the wealth and opulence that others lived in. The British might kowtow before their royals, people might fawn over celebrities and corporate giants, but not Randolph. Whatever class consciousness others possessed had withered and died inside Randolph when he was a little boy. If people had more than you, then it was there to be taken or destroyed. As the business with Manticore had shown, Randolph was a giant killer. The bigger they were, the harder they fell.

That being said, you could judge a fish by the size of the pond they swam in and, as he and Nicole walked arm in arm into Vito's private suites at the Grand Hotel, Oslo, he was struck with the realisation that Vito was in all likelihood a bloody big fish.

Nicole held onto him a little tighter. Randolph patted her arm. "Wow," he said, laughing. "This place is nice."

His port was automatically searching out information on the furniture and fittings and tags (and price tags) popped up in his field of vision. The huge suite was neo-classical, with frescoes in a Pompeian style. Randolph didn't know what that meant but it's what his port told him.

There were other guests in the room. Men and women. Players, partygoers and hangers-on. And more than a few suited bodyguards who were trying to blend in and mostly failing. Randolph had come here to play cards and make money, and he'd walked into a high class evening party instead. A bigger crowd, but the plan could stay essentially the same.

"Look at the parrots," said Nicole, pointing up.

There were at least half a dozen African grey parrots on brass stands around the edges of the room.

Randolph ported her a text message. *Fitted with ports no doubt. There will be people watching through those eyes.*

*Having second doubts?* she replied.

*I owe Payapapa-Papala too much.*

*How much?*

He frowned at her. How many times did she have to ask? Did she enjoy the pain of reminding him of the size of his debt? He owed the slimy bastard a lot of money and the only way he was going to pay it back was by ripping off other people with too much money.

"Where's the game?" Randolph said to Vito, grinning.

Vito Zwart, identified on his public profiles as simply 'a businessman' (which covered a multitude of sins) led them to a gaming table. There was a trio already sitting there, two women and a man. Vito gestured for Randolph to take a chair. The info-tag Randolph's port had put on the chair told him it had been originally made for the Royal Palace not a mile from here, and was worth more than the average Norwegian made in a month. If Randolph could hightail it out of there with a dozen such chairs he'd be halfway to paying off his debt.

He sat and greeted the others.

One of the women dealt from a card shoe. "Texas Hold 'Em," she said.

"You are American, yes?" the man asked Randolph.

"I travel around a lot."

"I met Randolph and his friend at a club on Rådhusgata," said Vito. "I'm not sure he told me where they were from."

He looked round for Nicole, but she was already working the room. Nicole was an ideal partner: smart, but not so smart as to start thinking for herself. She was beautiful enough to fit in anywhere, yet not so angelic as to draw unwanted attention. She moved through the party crowd in her white gold dress, sipping champagne from a Moser crystal flute (the flute was worth a week's wages. The port wasn't smart enough to recognise and price the liquid inside).

Hands were played; together Randolph and Nicole cheated. It was not an elaborate system, but it was a skilful and effective one. Nicole was mostly there as his canary in the mine, to tell him if she thought the con was going south. Nicole circled the room, and if she happened to see anyone's pocket cards, she'd silently port the details to Randolph. But anyone could do that. And anyone could pay for a chipped fly or creepy-crawly and watch its visual feed; although getting a fly to look at a playing card long enough to clearly read its face was kind of tricky. Randolph didn't bother with hopping into the heads of insects. He cheated by hopping, unnoticed, into the heads of his fellow players.

Brain ports had been around for years, but only with the most recent Manticore innovations could people experience other people's sensory feeds, port to port. Randolph was that most detestable and skilled of creatures: a bodyhacker, a puppeteer.

Randolph looked at his cards and the flops cards in the centre of the table. He sat back in his chair, elbow on the armrest, fist under his chin to support it, and slid straight across to the red haired woman, Mrs Salvo. Out of her eyes he saw she had an ace and jack off suit. He bounced back within half a second. She didn't even know he'd been inside her head.

People assumed the standard firewalls and protection software were sufficient to keep them safe, and they were dead wrong. The real trick was breaking into someone's sensory feed without them noticing, doing it fast enough that your own, momentarily unconscious body didn't draw suspicion by dropping to the floor, drooling.

In short order, Randolph had dipped in and out of Mrs Salvo, Ms Stoltenberg, Mr Næss and his host Vito Zwart. It provided him with enough information to fold on the first round before the river card was turned. He made sure he won slowly, in increments, throwing away the occasional good hand before bluffing out players with a shoddy pair of pocket cards.

It was cheating. It was illegal. But Payapapa-Papala was

an unrelenting creditor. Given the choice between some light thievery and having his bones broken one by one while Payapapa-Papala watched from his tank with those alien eyes of his, Randolph was going to choose light thievery every time.

As midnight approached, Randolph had the biggest pile of chips on the table. He hadn't cleaned anyone out. You clean people out, they start to think there might be a reason. The notion they might just be a poor poker player kind of gets lost in the emotions. When they paused for drinks, Randolph reckoned in another hour he'd have raked in an optimal amount. A good night's work.

There was a winking notification in the corner of his mind, a call from Spike. Randolph wasn't sure he wanted to speak to Spike at the moment.

Nicole slipped in beside him as he rose from the table. "Enjoying yourself, sweetheart?" he said.

She held him close as he walked towards the bathrooms. "It's been fun watching you work."

"Team effort," he said. "You saw Vito's pocket nines. Your share going straight to Danni again?"

"Danni?" She looked away, momentarily distracted. "Yeah, yeah. Of course."

Nicole's sister was waiting on a neurological augmentation that would reverse her motor neurone disease. At least that was what Nicole told him. It was either a noble cause or a noble lie.

"I gotta—" Randolph jerked his thumb to the toilets.

"Sure," she said.

One of the chipped parrots squawked at Randolph as he

walked past. The security guy opposite gave it a look and a grunt. Randolph momentarily wondered what those beefy ex-military bodyguards thought about having their marketplace eroded by chipped animals and robots. The day humans found a way to actually bodyhack and control animals rather than just ride along, would be the day these grunts would find themselves out of work. Not that Randolph had any kind of sympathy for them. He'd been on the negative end of encounters with hired thugs.

He accepted the call from Spike as he went into a bathroom and locked the door behind him. "What do you want?" He went to the sink to look at himself in the mirror.

"*Is that any way to greet an old friend?*"

"We're friends?"

"*I've been asked to offer you a job.*"

Randolph paused washing his hands. Spike worked for Payapapa-Papala.

"Payapapa-Papala wants to offer me a job? I thought he was more interested in having my limbs ripped off."

"*Mr Eight sees this as a way of working off your debt.*"

"He doesn't like it when you call him that."

"*I'm not the one in his bad books.*"

"Then, yeah, hit me up for the job," said Randolph. "Where do you want me?"

"*The UAE – Abu Dhabi. By tomorrow morning.*"

Randolph dabbed water on his face. Technically, it was already tomorrow morning and Oslo was six thousand kilometres from Abu Dhabi. He shook his head. "I got this deal going on right now. I'm going to get the boss his money another way."

"*Okay,*" said Spike. "*Enobarbus said you wouldn't be able to do it.*"

"Enobarbus? What's that slimy morality-free second-rate bodyhacker got to do with this? He's a smash and grab thug. Not a puppeteer at all."

In Randolph's head, there was the port's emulation of Spike laughing. "*It's funny. You two are so quick to stick the knife into each other. The emotions! You should start dating.*"

"He's not half the artiste I am."

"*I know,*" said Spike, still chortling. "*That's why I'm just checking that you're not available. And you say you're not, so...*"

"But why does he think I wouldn't be? It's..."

There was a ported message from Nicole. *You coming out? They're ready to restart.*

"Gotta go, Spike." He killed the call. He dried his hands and face, checked his bow-tie in the mirror, and headed out.

Randolph rarely had nightmares. Part of the talent of the true puppeteer was having total control over one's thoughts and mental faculties. Dreams were something Randolph could detect and lucidly control. But that didn't mean he'd never had nightmares. People talk about nightmares in which you turn up for the exam or the big speech, and discover you're naked. Randolph had never experienced that particular dream – nakedness had never been a source of embarrassment for him – but it was a variant of the group of dreams in which the dreamer was the odd one out. The zombie nightmare, the Invasion of the Body Snatchers nightmare. The fear that everyone else in the world was aware of you and despised you.

Randolph came back into the main suite and walked

straight into that nightmare. Two dozen guests, a dozen bouncers, and a flock of beady-eyed parrots all looked at him. There was no music. There was no chatter. Only the silence and the staring.

"Here he is," said Vito, gesturing dramatically at Randolph and drawing smiles from the guests.

"Um," said Randolph, which wasn't suave or intelligent, but was a fair reflection of his mental state.

"We've just discovered that young Randolph here has been systematically robbing us to the tune of—" Vito ran a hand through the chips nearest to him on the table. "—a million krona?"

Randolph coughed and forced a smile. Simultaneously, he launched the *PIZZA BOMB* protocol from his port. He scanned the room for Nicole. Where the hell was she?

"Vito," he said. "I know you've been losing. And drinking. And I've been very lucky."

"Oh, don't embarrass yourself further," said Vito, who was clearly enjoying the moment. "We have proof."

One of the hired thugs, part of that dying breed not yet made redundant by technology, took hold of Randolph's arm. Randolph was a young and fit guy but he was built for speed, not violence.

A hand brushed his other arm. Nicole had sidled up next to him.

"Nicole, tell these people. We're not – I'm mean I'm not a cheat."

Nicole laughed. She had a lovely laugh, the kind men liked, but right now, Randolph didn't appreciate the edge on it.

"It's so funny, Randy," she said. "You still think I'm Nicole."

Randolph stared fiercely into her eyes as though he could see straight into her mind and port. Only one person ever called him Randy.

"Enobarbus?"

Randolph had wondered how Enobarbus was so sure he wasn't going to be able to take that job in Abu Dhabi. A job which would have settled Randolph's debts for good – as would have the chips on the poker table. Right now, they both might as well be six thousand kilometres away.

## 2

Constance Wileman woke but she couldn't pinpoint the reason why.

She had been dreaming she was a meat avatar again. It was a familiar dream in which she was being fitted for a dress that would ultimately be worn by her patron, Alessa Durant. Her job was simply to stand and be dressed by the industrious swarm of couturiers and assistants. All the while, businesswoman and bon vivant Alessa Durant squatted in her head, telling her to look in the mirror, this way and that, while simultaneously demons (or it could have been Alessa herself; it was hard to tell in the dream) whispered she had gained weight and lost muscle tone. That she had deviated from the precise body template which Alessa had hired her to maintain. There was no point being a meat avatar if you didn't match the specification of your patron.

It wasn't so much a dream as a memory, or an amalgam of

memories, and certainly not enough to disturb Constance from her sleep.

Her port told her there was a call waiting. It was Helen Akindele, another of the Alessa survivors. Had there been some sort of bleed-through from her port to her dreams, a subconscious signal prompting the memory? Constance doubted it. The dream was common enough to be boring, and Constance was enough of an expert in brainport neuroscience to know that, barring a software error, such things didn't happen. However, the question was an interesting one and only served to wake her up further.

Softly cursing, she got out of bed, ported the bare minimum of lights to come on and went to the drinks bar by the window. She reached for the robe on the chair. Even though she had notional control of the temperature, the hotel room seemed hellbent on air conditioning her half to death with a wintry breeze. Maybe in a country where the daytime temperature could frequently top fifty degrees, the AC liked to remind you how much you depended on it.

Constance cracked open a small bottle of mineral water and stood at the floor length window to look out over the resort zoo below. At three in the morning, the city was illuminated by lines of yellow and blue light, determined to show it had energy to burn. However, the zoo directly below the hotel was dark, and the canopy of trees over the ape enclosure was just a mat of darker blues and shadow. Down there was Damba, her gorilla – not that the gorilla belonged to her, more that her fortunes were tied to him. She hoped he was sleeping well. The journey from the forest research station in Uganda had been stressful for him, and Damba had a big day tomorrow, with some important investors to impress.

Tomorrow was today, she thought, and groaned at herself for being awake when she should be asleep. She clicked the call from Helen Akindele. The Alessa Survivors – that's what they called themselves; there were twelve of them so far – had formed an informal support group. There was an unspoken agreement they would always be there for each other.

"Morning, Helen," said Constance.

"*Shit. What time is it there?*" said Helen.

"It doesn't matter." According to her public profile, Helen was in New York. It was evening there. "How's things?"

"*My therapist tells me I have an eating disorder.*"

"Uh-huh?"

"*You're not going to disagree with her?*"

"Are you still measuring yourself every day and cutting your calories accordingly?"

"*That's not a disorder. That's just habit.*"

"I hear that."

Constance had been a meat avatar for Alessa for two years, two years in which she had to exercise, diet and binge to maintain a body profile identical to her patron. The measuring, the eating and the exercise had been a daily routine. The concept was simple. Here is a body outline, a template, a doorway with a precise hole cut in it. You have to match it perfectly to be able to step through to the other side where the money is.

"But you're not an avatar anymore," Constance pointed out. Softly, because she'd said it often enough.

"*I know that,*" said Helen, "*but what am I supposed to do? Just stop?*"

Constance nodded even though no one could see. Out on the dark highway by the coast, red and white lights raced each other. "You know what I did when I quit as an avatar?"

"*Ate hamburgers every day until you'd gained ten pounds,*" said Helen. "*I know.*"

Constance had had so many conversations with the Alessa Survivors that she repeated herself a lot. And was it terrible that, sometimes, she struggled to differentiate between the newer ones. At least Constance was lucky to have worked for, and occasionally as, Alessa before the point when Alessa began to insist her avatars had facial reconstruction to match her look precisely.

How's the—" Constance glanced at the port notes she had on Helen "—the journalism work going?"

"*I gave up on that. Human journalism can't compete with the bots. They don't need to sleep and they don't struggle to think of synonyms for 'really really cool.' The bots are writing the fashion journalism, and they're designing the clothes too. Last year's Fashion Week, less than half the garments were human-designed. They only need us to wear them and buy them. You used your avatar fees to put yourself through college. I shoulda done that.*"

"Not college exactly. I did it to pay for my research project."

"*Studying animal brains, or something like that?*"

"Something like that," Constance agreed. "So if you're not going into journalism then...?"

"*Ugh.*" It was a sound of contempt. "*I don't know. I did think of asking Alessa's team if they'd want me back.*"

"Really?" said Constance and regretted the judgemental tone of her voice.

*"It's the one thing I've been good at."*

"That's not true."

*"You don't know me. I may have just been a glove puppet for a rich woman too scared to leave the house—"*

"Hey."

*"—meaning no more to her than the clothes I wear for her or the parties I attend in her name, but at least she looks after her things, you know? It's not like she bodyhacks me and takes over. She hasn't got the talent for that."*

Constance thought about the presentation she and the other Symbio guys were going to give in the morning. Their work was with great apes, but the applications for human-to-human work would be just around the corner. "Maybe you should think about living your own life now."

*"Maybe that's what I'm saying. Maybe I don't have one of my own. There's that fable."*

"Fable?"

*"I think so. About a dog and a wolf. The wolf tells the dog to come away with it to live wild and free, and the dog runs away from its safe little home and ends up in the woods where a pack of wolves then eat it."*

"Nice fable."

*"I think my mum read it to me as a bedtime story."*

Constance automatically looked up fables about dogs and wolves and found stories with quite opposite moral meanings.

*"You've got your amazing science job,"* said Helen. *"Some of us don't have that."*

"Big science job, huh? If the guys at the meeting tomorrow don't like our big science project then I might be without a job. Let loose among the wolves." Tiredness was making her poetic.

*"Shit. What time is it where you are?"*

"It doesn't matter," said Constance and immediately yawned.

*"I'll leave you. Gotta go,"* said Helen and ended the call.

The call vanishing was like a string being cut. Constance could feel her body instantly sag and her tired eyes drift out of focus. The lights of the city smeared across her vision.

# 3

The slab of walking muscle had Randolph's arm securely. Vito could see that and appeared to be in no hurry dealing with Randolph. Vito had brought a dirty little commoner to the ritzy party, and now his cheating was uncovered, the partygoers looked inclined to have a little sport with him. In a world of people living lives of safe and vicarious thrills, having a genuine bodyhacker and thief among them was rare entertainment value.

The police had been called. How quickly they'd be here, in the middle of a cold autumn night, was uncertain. Randolph checked the time. He'd launched the pizza bomb program three minutes ago.

"Do you do this often?" Vito was asking.

"Get roughly manhandled by burly Norwegians?" Randolph replied. "Because my friend's been bodyhacked by an amoral jerk and forced to spout lies about me?"

"Oh, he's so good," said Vito, playing to the crowd. "He can't stop lying."

"Randolph J. Howard," said Nicole (or rather Enobarbus said, at the controls of her brain). "Born in Santa Clara, California. Educated at Wilcox High School before going onto Stanford University before dropping out without—"

"Doxing me?" said Randolph. "Spouting my life story in public? Why don't you tell them my parents' address so they can send letters of admo—"

"Two three eight five Homestead Road. Mr and Mrs—"

"Come on!" Randolph shouted. "Not cool, man. Seriously."

Randolph could pretend to be angry. He was good at that too. Mr Dimwich at Wilcox High said Randolph had a fine gift for the dramatic arts. Dimwich hadn't been his drama teacher. He was the janitor, and had said this to the Principal following Randolph's histrionics after being caught stealing cleaning supplies. But a compliment was a compliment. Randolph could be pretend to be angry – the fact he was really angry also helped.

While he ranted and bickered, he was scoping out the room, both physically and digitally. Physically, he was surrounded by party guests. The exit from the suit was fifty feet away, through a small but dense crowd, and across a long dining table with a banquet-sized buffet laid out on it. A better and more achievable exit was through the glass doors leading out onto a side terrace. There was still a wall of high-class guests in the way though, and a brutish bouncer holding him.

Digitally, the crowd was the usual smorgasbord of variable

security levels. There wasn't a single person in the room without a brainport – he'd have been surprised if there had been. Only loonies and anti-tech zealots didn't have them. While some people had decent enough tech security, too many assumed the default firewall protection which came with their ports was enough to keep them safe. Randolph sought out one he would be able to hack and then – not just occupy, looking out of their eyes and listening through their ears – seize control of for a moment. All he would need was a moment.

There was a knock at the main door and the sounds of a muffled commotion. It was either the police, or the pizza bomb. Whichever, now was the moment to act. Someone went to open the door. A member of hotel staff entered and then, with a yell of surprise, failed to stop a line of flying drones follow him in, all with flat cardboard boxes slung beneath them.

"*Pizza for Vito!*" declared the lead drone electronically.

Oslo, Randolph had read, had the highest concentration of pizza restaurants per capita of any city in the world. The sudden arrival of – Randolph didn't stop to count – thirty or more delivery drones, all with the same script-driven order to deliver a margherita pizza to one Vito Zwart at this location, was his cue.

As people turned, Randolph leaped into the nearby body of a waiter carrying a tray of drinks. In the most meanly hasty bodyhack he'd done in a while, he seized control of the young man's body via brainport routes that were never designed to work in two directions, and launched him at the security guy holding Randolph. Caught by surprise, the

security guy was toppled into a table, losing his grip on
Randolph.

Randolph jumped back to his own body before it fell
comatose and driverless to the floor. There were shouts.
There were screams. There was a hell of a lot of pizza.
Drones were whirling around at head height, their anti-
collision protocols spinning them into little insect dances
with one another. Almost no one was watching Randolph.

He leapt for the glass doors, forcing himself between
stunned partygoers. The doors weren't locked, which was a
blessing.

The night air was a blast of cold. It took Randolph's eyes a
second to adjust to the dark. Ahead there was a short iron
railing fence against a screening row of short conifer trees.
Left to right ran the path skirting the exterior of the hotel.
Randolph headed right, toward the front of the hotel and the
street.

"Randy!"

That was a man's voice. Randolph glanced back. A bald
guy in a tux stood at the open door. Was that Enobarbus
himself? No, of course not. Enobarbus had just head-hopped
into a convenient victim. A drone, out of control, flew out the
door, bounced off the bald man's head and buried itself in
the conifer hedge.

Randolph ran on. There was the whoop of police sirens
and the flash of blue lights ahead. He couldn't see the
vehicles, just the lights, reflecting off bushes and stonework.
He jinked left, jumped the short fence and dived blindly
through the hedge. He landed badly on the sidewalk among

snapped branches. His foot sort of went from under him and he nearly twisted his ankle. Nearly.

He picked himself up and ran. He ran south, down a pedestrianised road between a park and the Norwegian parliament building. His port gifted him unhelpful data about the building's history and architecture which he swiped away.

There were shouts behind. He heard running footsteps. He ran through a narrow curving street between square high-rise buildings and as he ran his port searched for a car he could hire. Any vehicle at all. Midnight in Oslo and there was nothing within range.

*"Hei!"* shouted a voice.

He glanced back. One of the slabs of muscle from the party was coming after him. The man's face was tomato red as he ran, surround by breath clouded by the freezing air. Randolph didn't stop to wonder if this was Enobarbus again, riding a hijacked victim and not caring if he gave the man a heart attack.

Randolph stumbled past a young couple and ran down Rosenkrantz Gate. His pursuer gave a shout and spilled into the road. The young couple went to him. Almost immediately the young man turned and ran after Randolph. Despite what Randolph had said to Spike, Enobarbus could leap from body to body with a grace Randolph couldn't match.

He swerved around a tram along the port front.

His port pinged with a search solution. He would have laughed if he wasn't so out of breath. He had asked for any vehicle after all. He booked it immediately. It was only a few hundred metres from his location.

He pushed forward on aching legs.

The *Oslo Tours and Excursions* boat was by the quayside. A white tourist thing for maybe twenty passengers. Randolph used the last of his money to hire the whole thing, pinging it with a message.

*Trip to Hovedøya or Lindøya?,* it replied automatically.

*Just start the engines*, he shot back. *Leaving now.*

He skidded on the smooth stone of the quay as he swung round to board it. There was no crew in sight. Cars were driverless. Why not boats? The thought had never occurred to him before.

The engines were running, the gangplank retracting automatically but it was slow to pull away from the quay. Randolph leaned – mostly crashed – against the wall of the passenger cabin and heaved and coughed as he tried to get his breath back. The air was ice needles in his throat. He watched the quay, but neither Enobarbus nor the police came for him.

He moved inside and found a communication post where he could talk to the boat directly.

"Okay. Take me to the airport," he said.

*"The airport is fifty kilometres inland,"* said the boat. *"Are you being serious, sir?"*

"Figure it out." Randolph collapsed into a seat, looking through flight options to Abu Dhabi before telling Spike he would take the job.

# 4

Sleep eluded Constance for the rest of the night. She might have lain on the bed with her eyes closed and drifted off into some sort of thoughtless state, but it wasn't sleep. Before the dawn, she was up and heading downstairs to go for a jog. She asked the man on reception for suggested routes.

"We have a fully equipped gym on site," he said, surprised Constance would want to run outside.

"I need to blow the cobwebs away," she said.

"Blow cobwebs?" said the receptionist. He twitched as he accessed a translation. "Do you need your room cleaning?"

"Never mind," said Constance, heading for the door anyway.

"You should use the gym, madam," the receptionist called after her but she ignored him.

The sun rose quickly as she jogged round the perimeter of the zoological park attached to the hotel. The sounds of birds and other animals greeting the new day mingled with the light wind in the trees.

Back in the days when she'd been a meat avatar for Alessa Durant, it had all been about the exercise and the diet. She'd even subcontracted some of the exercise to an agency. For four hours a week, she'd invite an agent into her head to take over her gross motor function and run, swim and aerobicise her body into shape, while Constance sat back and just concentrated on the benefits this outsourced torture provided. The body sculptor (yes, that was what they called themselves) was a woman called Pearl who never communicated directly. Constance suspected they used a variety of people who all used the name Pearl. She had no idea where the body sculptors actually were. LA? New Delhi? Working out of a government internment facility in China? She'd read somewhere that some body sculpting agencies didn't even pay their agents, just using individuals who got a kick out of putting a younger, more attractive body through its paces. Constance generally ignored sensationalised and unevidenced claims.

Sweaty and exhausted, she returned to the hotel and waved at the receptionist as she passed. Was that a look of disgusted disdain he gave her? She went to her room to shower and dress. There was a little momentary crisis when she wondered what one wore to sell one's life's work to corporate investors, but she had brought limited clothing options with her from the research station in Kampala.

She went down to the restaurant for breakfast. Krish and Martin were already there, taking up a large table between the pair of them. They looked as though they'd been there a while. Krish Sethi, Symbio's head of media and investment relations, stood and beckoned Constance over.

She feared what conversations had already gone on between them. While Martin was the founder of the company and CEO, Symbio had been built upon research work which Constance had started at university. She was the better scientist, Martin the visionary and the boss. Krish, meanwhile, had a propensity for spouting bullshit that tended to upset and derail Martin's general line of thinking. Nonetheless, the CEO was going to rely heavily on both of them during this crucial meeting: Krish for his sales ability and showmanship, Constance for making sure they were on course with their overall business strategy.

Constance joined them. A waitress met her at the table. Constance asked her to bring coffee.

"Can I just say," said the waitress, beaming, "you look just like that famous woman. You know, the businesswoman."

"Alessa Durant?"

"Yes!"

"No, I don't," said Constance and sat down to join the preparations for the big day.

## 5

"Was it Arthur C Clarke who said communication technology was the enemy of transport technology?" said Randolph, passing his bag to Spike in the arrivals lounge of Abu Dhabi International Airport.

"What?"

Spike was a slight chap. He had wild hair which seemed too much for his diminutive frame to carry, and Randolph's travel bag weighed him down even though it only contained things he'd bought at Oslo Airport.

"Hardly anyone flies anywhere anymore," said Randolph, waving his hand round at the airport. "Why does anyone fly if you can 'port anywhere, virtually, for a fraction of the cost?"

"I dunno," said Spike. "Did he say it? You could look it up."

Randolph could and involuntarily did. That was the

problem with brain ports, the problem with any tool. Put a car's steering wheel in front of someone and they instinctively drove everywhere. Put a gun in someone's hand and they instinctively fired it. Give a man a brain port and he never thought for himself ever again.

Randolph twitched in irritation at himself as Clarke quotes about space and aliens and magic washed over him.

"Communication technology is the enemy of conversation, that's for certain."

"You sound cranky," said Spike. "Flight boring?"

Randolph didn't answer: just walked towards the car pool. The retail units near the exit were dominated by tourist companies.

FREE DIVE IN THE PERSIAN GULF FROM THE SAFETY OF YOUR SUN LOUNGER, suggested one ad screen on which a blonde in an asymmetrical bikini, beads of water glistening on her skin, smouldered to camera. It was ridiculous. Why would any holidaymaker make the tedious physical journey here only to chicken out and take the virtual option at the last moment? Randolph knew the answer, of course. The attraction was not the free diving; the attraction was free diving as passenger in that young beauty's body. The blonde on the screen half-reminded Randolph of a classic film, a spy movie. He clamped down hard on the urge to get his brain port to fill in the gaps.

A car trundled towards them as they exited. Spike dumped the bag on a seat and ported their destination to the car. Randolph checked it.

"Al Bahyah Park Resort Hotel?"

"That's the one," said Spike. "The target is also in the

hotel."

Randolph nodded. "Timescale?"

Spike looked at a watch he wasn't wearing. Either it was an archaic mime or he had indulgently set his port to project the time onto his wrist.

"Ideally, we want you to make the jump in the next half hour."

"What? That's no time at all."

"Mr Eight called you in as soon as the window of opportunity became available."

"He doesn't like it if you call him that."

"He doesn't know I call him that, and no one can pronounce his real name."

"Payapapa-Papala does not like it when you call him Mister Eight. And half an hour is no time at all to prepare for a jump. Hijacking human bodies isn't like ... like jacking a car." Randolph sighed irritably and looked out of the window at the sun-baked city rolling by. A swarm of insects swirled over a rooftop, then flew in along the road behind them.

"Oh, I see," said Spike. "I thought you were the best puppeteer in the business. I was mistaken, was I?"

"Don't try to appeal to my professional pride," said Randolph. "There's no excuse for poor planning and haven't forgotten you almost hired Enobarbus."

The swarm of insects followed them for half a mile before peeling away. It was possible that, in some darkened control room, a law enforcement officer watching the feed from the swarm had momentarily seen the scowl on Randolph's face as the insects flew past.

# 6

"What the hell is this?" asked Constance.

Krish paused in the act of laying out Symbio brochures around a table. The meeting was set up in one of the resort hotel's dining rooms, chosen because it overlooked the wildlife park's primate enclosure.

"What?" he said.

Constance recognised the importance of having a live subject at the pitch meeting, but that didn't mean she had to like it. She'd made sure Damba's welfare was uppermost in everyone's minds, that he had a private and natural enclosure in the park for this presentation. So when she saw a cage had been installed inside the conference room, she knew it could only be Krish's handiwork.

Constance went over to the cage where Damba the silverback mountain gorilla sat, his back to the room, toying miserably with strands of hay.

"What is this?" she demanded. "I thought it was very clear we are not putting on a freak show here. The enclosure next door is where Damba should be, not here in this air-conditioned hell with everyone staring at him."

"Relax," said Krish, in a tone that suggested she was the unreasonable one. "He won't be in here for the whole time. It's just for that wow factor when everyone arrives." Krish did jazz hands, presumably to illustrate what a wow factor looked like, but really demonstrating what a twat looked like.

Constance stabbed the itinerary on her tablet with a finger. "There's a tour included, so that everyone gets to see him. In his enclosure. Which we hired for that specific purpose. He does *not* need to be in the room. He'll feel threatened and it will make him stressed."

"A tour won't take people's breath away," said Krish. "It'll just be like visiting a zoo. Don't worry, I got the handlers to sign off on this cage. It's got privacy glass around it, so that Damba won't even see everyone looking. It's all fine, Constance."

She shook her head. "You should have consulted me."

Krish gave her a blankly indifferent look. "Did I insist you and Martin consult with me when you were doing all the science stuff? No. I let you do your job. Let me do mine."

It was too late to insist upon moving Damba before the meeting started, simply because of the logistics of transporting a silverback gorilla around a hotel. Krish must have had the team up early to get him in here via the service elevator.

She distracted herself by updating the agenda for the day

to remove the tour, then she made sure that Martin and Krish were up to speed with who was doing what.

An alert popped up on Constance's tablet and chimed from her brain port at the same time. "The investors have arrived. I'll go and escort them in. We're good to go, yes?"

## 7

The traffic ahead slowed. Local police had stopped a truck and trailer. Police dogs were searching under the trailer while officers questioned the human driver. The dogs wore combat armour harnesses and shoulder-mounted weaponry. They couldn't fire the weapons of course, that would be down to whatever ported human was riding along inside them. Nonetheless, there was something about the thought of dogs with guns that unnerved Randolph.

He didn't like being stuck in traffic either.

Sometimes, Randolph missed the days when he could actually drive a car, manually, physically drive it. There was an adrenaline rush to be got from taking risks, driving too fast or too close. All part of the game. Of course, things were better now. Cars were better off driving themselves – they were safer, there were fewer gridlocks and letting the car do all of the work freed up journey time for other things.

But right now Randolph wished he could drive. They were ten minutes from the hotel. "Okay. Tell me about the target."

Spike ported him the data, a packet at a time, teasing it out like a slide presentation. "Symbio Technology," he said.

"Never heard of them," said Randolph.

"You wouldn't have. They're a tiny research company at the moment with some tech Mr Eight really wants to get his hands on."

"Hands?"

"Symbio has a three-person team in the city doing a pitch to venture capitalist investors. The investors will enable them to go from research project to full scale production. These are the same investors who bought up the remnants of Manticore after you gutted—"

"I know what I did to Manticore. Move on."

"Mr Eight wants you to port in, steal the tech, and bring it out to me."

"And you'll be sitting in a car round the back, waiting. The usual drill."

"A reinforced security van actually. For reasons that will become apparent."

Randolph flicked between the images of the Symbio team. "Which one am I porting into?"

Spike grinned and ported him the next film.

Randolph stared. "Who the fuck is Damba?"

"Damba is—"

"I can see who Damba is, Spike," he growled. "Let me rephrase. Damba is a fucking ape. I can't hijack an animal body. I can no more insert myself into an animal's mind than

I can fit into a baby's ... what do you call those all in one things babies wear?"

Spike shrugged. "Boiler suit?"

"It's not a bloody boiler suit. Like a onesie. A romper suit. One of them. It can't be done. I can't hijack a gorilla."

"You can," said Spike. "And that's why this tech is so valuable. Here. Watch this." He ported a video to Randolph.

# 8

The investors came in with Martin. There were three men and three women. The men wore expensive suits without ties, loose and casual, like male models on perfume adverts; except these guys didn't have the style or physiques to be any kind of model, so the casual formal look kind of gave them an 'uncle on the wedding dance floor' vibe. Martin was doing that loud and garrulous thing he did in company. Privately, he was a gentle and quiet man. Put him in an enforced social situation and he became a man of big false laughs and big physical gestures. The kind of thing that worked perfectly with these types.

The local women who came in with them were young, slender, entirely expressionless and silent. Body hosts, Constance decided. Meat avatars. Inside each an investor or lawyer or some such was hitching a ride, porting in to pick up the sensory feed of that person, hearing and seeing what was going on in the meeting.

Martin tore himself away from the laughter and joviality and gestured to Constance and Krish. "The other members of our triumvirate at Symbio. Krish and Constance."

The men crowded forward to shake Krish's hand. Two immediately moved on to look at Damba in his glass cage. The third nodded a greeting to Constance but, with a half-hearted gesture to the table between them, did not come round to shake her hand.

"Our three guests," said Martin. "Don, Dom—"

"And they call me Bozza," said the one nearest Damba's cage, saying it like he defied anyone to laugh.

The silent body hosts took seats on chairs near the wall.

"Not worried about hackers snooping on us?" said Krish, pointing at the body hosts. He said it like a joke but there was a serious edge.

Dom put a hand on the shoulder of one of the hosts. The young woman didn't even blink. "We have the best security in place. We utilise unbeatable firewall and anti-malware products."

Martin grinned. "Don, Dom and Bozza are part of the investment consortium that bought out Manticore after—" He winced, realising he didn't want to say that 'after'. Everyone knew what that 'after' signified.

Bozza laughed. "It's all, right mate. After Manticore went tits up, right?" He had a sort of free-floating, non-British English accent. It veered slightly towards South African and then away to something approximating Australian, with a kind of free-ranging international twang. "Manticore ballsed it up and we picked up the pieces."

Constance nodded politely in acknowledgement. Manticore had been a world leader in sensory communication. They had taken the tech created by the initial brain port companies and used it to enable sensory input streaming, allowing people to ride along with volunteer body hosts anywhere in the world. Want to skydive with your feet on the ground? Want to dance with the Bolshoi Ballet company? Want to drive a stunt car over a dozen buses? Manticore's tech allowed you to do just that. Manticore gave the world the internet of human sensation and, of course, as with most new tech, people quickly worked out how to use it for sexual gratification. Although it was never acknowledged in the advertising, Manticore could not deny that their meteoric corporate rise was due to people having disease and mostly guilt free proxy-sex in younger and sexier bodies than their own.

Manticore, innovators rather than creators, had rapidly given the world what it had never realised it wanted. Manticore's failure – and it was a catastrophic one – was not realising others would want to exploit that. Bodyhackers entered the arena. Manticore's business operated on a model of willing body hosts allowing passive passengers into their minds. The two key words being 'willing' and 'passive'. These were such a given that they weren't even discussed until the bodyhackers pointed out the distinction. Manticore's biggest sin was perhaps not developing the security measures to ensure only invited guests could drop in for a visit. A skilled bodyhacker would bypass the inadequate firewalls and ride unnoticed. Bodysurfing became an illicit passion with its own subculture. Some of it was essentially innocent. Constance recalled a story of an American woman who had a virtual phrogger living in her head for two years, unnoticed. But then there was the downright creepy and dangerous stuff – bodyhackers squatting in people's heads while they access their encrypted finances, trying to hack celebrity brain ports, or hack the brain ports of military or security personnel. There was even an unfounded rumour that at one point, state-sponsored terrorist organisations had a bodyhacker in the ministerial officers of every European nation.

Manticore imploded within the space of weeks. They'd built a doorway into people's heads, and the public rightly revolted when the burglars came pouring in. And that was even before the rumours that some bodyhackers had developed techniques to take control of their hosts were proven to be true. When it was discovered that passive passengers could, theoretically, become active controllers, people started ripping the ports out of their heads.

Puppeteers were scary and real and, at once, the most reviled people in society.

## 9

Randolph watched the video Spike had sent him. With a voiceover explaining how many threats were faced by the great apes of the world, there were apocalyptic scenes of bulldozers, fires and scorched earth replacing rainforest, spliced with mother orang-utans, chimps and gorillas cradling their babies and trying to flee the horror which surrounded them.

*How can we get these animals to sanctuary? When they recognise the threat, it's already too late.*

The tone of the video changed at that point. To a soundtrack of uplifting music, a team of friendly-faced scientists studied a map of Uganda and videos of gorillas. A particular gorilla was the focus.

*Damba is the alpha male. The rest of the troop will follow him to safety. This is why Damba has been implanted with a Symbio port.*

This was followed by one of the scientists reclining in a seat with sensors attached to various points on his head.

*By taking temporary control of Damba, we can rescue the entire troop with minimal stress to the animals. We are happy to report that these field trials were a resounding success. All of the gorillas were moved and they are now living happily in a protected area of rainforest.*

*We want to make this technology available wherever it's needed. No great ape should have to die. With the help of Symbio ports, we can safeguard their future forever.*

Randolph swiped the video away. "That's not meant to be possible."

"I know," said Spike.

The car had drawn up outside the Al Bahyah Park Resort Hotel. Randolph stepped out and took his bag with him. "Puppetry is not easy," he said.

"I know," said Spike.

It struck people as obvious that controlling someone else's body should be as easy as controlling your own. It wasn't. It really wasn't. To think that way was to assume that navigating someone else's home would be as easy as navigating your own. Everyone's home had a place to sleep, a place to eat, a place to shit, shower and shave. But no two homes were alike and bodies were far more idiosyncratic. Different body shapes, different muscle strengths, different sensory variations. That slight in-turning of your foot you'd lived with all your life? That twinge in your neck you'd had so long you'd forgotten it was even there? That minor deafness? That colour-blindness? Those tiny quirks and imperfections which were so tiny they couldn't even be named? To a bodyhacker blindly taking control, those idiosyncrasies of a human body would be enough to overwhelm them and leave them as a quivering wreck on the floor.

"Even things we think of as universal experiences are nothing of the sort."

"I know," said Spike. "First time I tried, I thought red was green for a week." He went up to the receptionist. You could tell this was a five star hotel; they still employed humans for the role. "We have a booking. Name of Dennett."

"Your suite is ready," said the receptionist.

Spike twitched as the receptionist ported the room access codes to him. "Actually, it's my friend who's staying here."

The receptionist ported the room codes and hotel information to Randolph. The suite was on the twelfth floor with a balcony overlooking the resort park.

"I want to make sure one last time," said Randolph. "I'm keeping irregular hours, and I don't want to be disturbed. Housekeeping may not enter my room. Please reassure me that this is understood."

"Yes sir, it is clear," said the receptionist.

They went to the lifts. Spike had already called one and they rode up with the lift to themselves.

"You can't bodyhack and control an animal," said Randolph, getting back to his major concern. "No more than a rabbit can speak Swahili. The neurological pathways. The brain architecture. The goddamn physical infrastructure."

"And this is what Symbio has apparently bypassed," said Spike. "Their port isn't just a connection device. It's a living and learning interpreter."

"Living?" said Randolph.

Spike nodded. "Nano-built synthetic life. It's not a regular port. You can't just pop down to your local tattoo and piercing parlour and have one implanted. It is seeded and grows in the host—"

Randolph pulled a face. "Not sure I fancy that."

"—which also means we can't just steal the schematics or rip out the port unit. Mr Eight needs the Symbio port, which also means he needs the port host."

"The gorilla."

"The gorilla."

"Hence the reinforced security van out back."

"Right."

The lift binged to let them know it had arrived, which was a quaint touch. The booked suite was a short distance down the corridor. Randolph ported the door to unlock and they walked straight in. Despite having told the receptionist already, he ported the room systems to keep the door locked at all times and hung a big virtual Do Not Disturb sign on the door.

Randolph saw the body-sculpted reclining chair which he had requested during the night flight from Oslo had been delivered.

"Is that thing strictly necessary?" said Spike.

"Nope," grinned Randolph. "But damned if I'm not going to be comfortable while I do this."

"You get a kick out of being pandered to."

"You noticed?"

He put his bag on the bed and looked over the equipment Spike had procured. It included the IV line and catheter, both essential for keeping him hydrated, nourished and accident-free if the mission ran to more than a few hours.

"The target, Damba, is in an enclosure in the park," said Spike. "You've got his port identifiers. I gather these Symbio ports give out a fuzzier locator signal, but it's a zoo and it's the only Symbio port there. You've got the maps of the park. A gorilla body and Randolph's mind ... shouldn't be hard getting out to the service area of the hotel."

"Says the man who can't steer a human body to a man who is going to try to operate an ape for the first time."

"Mr Eight has great faith in you."

Randolph shook his head but smiled anyway. He waggled the catheter at Spike. "You going to stand and watch while I hook myself up?"

"I've seen you at your worst," said Spike. He dropped an audio and video globe on the desk and tapped it to turn it on. "I can perve on you from the safety of the van."

# 10

"As early as the twenty-tens, scientists were implanting brain prostheses in macaque monkeys," said Krish, warming to his pitch. "Cybernetically enhanced insects were being used as explosive detectors not much more than a decade later. DARPA followed up with remote-controlled sharks soon after. Those same sharks, enhanced with Jaffle brain ports, are patrolling our seas even today."

Bozza made to spit at the name 'Jaffle', as though the industry leader in brain ports was a dirty word.

"Manticore brought in sensory streaming more recently," Krish continued. "And, yes, it became possible to ride along in the mind and sensory experiences of all manner of living things. There were the entertainment possibilities. Who wouldn't want to not just swim with the dolphins, but swim *as* a dolphin? Experience the chaotic and confusing but undoubtedly fun adventures of a dog on the scent of something? But there were the practical applications. Getting the public to ride in the minds of Serengeti elephants. Entertainment for them, but also a means to spot poachers and then, once disengaged, to alert the authorities. Ivory poaching reduced to almost zero on Manticore's watch."

The investors nodded as though this was their own personal achievement, rather than something others had done before they scavenged the pieces of the disgraced company.

"But all the while, though we could be subjected to the raw sensations these animal experienced, there was a biological language barrier. We could never truly know what it was to be that animal or to even think about taking control. Until now..." Krish paused dramatically. In Constance's opinion, he always overdid it.

"But how does it work?" asked investor Dom.

"Symbio's patented neuro-alignment system means that the Symbio port translates the animal's unique somatic nervous system signals in a way that our own brain and nervous system can utilise. It is like – if you'll allow me an old fashioned analogy – like a travel adaptor plug, allowing you to use your own devices in a foreign country."

"But how does it work?" repeated Dom.

"When you invest with us and we begin full scale production," Martin cut in, "we will share all the technical specs."

"And let's be clear," said Krish. "The neuro-alignment makes it child's play to ride and drive *any* host body. So-called 'puppeteers' being the only ones able to master the art will become a thing of the past."

# 11

Randolph was ready. He'd lined up the software arsenal he needed for the hack. He reclined on his seat and brought up a map of data signatures in the local area. Damba's port was not in the park zoo. He zoomed out and found it closer to home, in the hotel itself. Most ports and data-points on the map were dot icons, but Damba's appeared as a diffused green stain, like it was neither one thing nor another. It bled into and masked the half dozen other signals in the immediate vicinity, but it was there nonetheless.

"Slide in, take a look, ride it out," he told himself. He smiled at the realisation that here was one bodyhack where, if it went wrong, the victim wouldn't be able to tell anyone what had happened.

Randolph didn't just leap in. He utilised breathing techniques to slow down his heart rate. It was important not to induce extra physical shock in the subject by turning up with any residual anxiety or bodily tension. It was certainly traumatic to relinquish control of one's brain to a temporary hijacker, but with this procedure there was a risk of heart attack if done carelessly. Obviously, no official codes of conduct existed for this type of activity, but his own research had established some of his personal rules of engagement.

Once truly relaxed, he used visualisation techniques to ready himself. They helped in two ways: firstly, Randolph firmly believed in the power of visualisation for reaching goals. He pictured himself comfortably inhabiting the body of the gorilla, escaping from its environment as the cage door was released with the scheduled hack he'd programmed. He would then steer it out of captivity and into the back of Spike's van. The second reason was to ease the transition. He practised looking through those deep-set eyes and flexing the muscles in those massive arms. By the time he was ready to press the trigger, he had fully pictured himself as a gorilla (or what he at least imagined being a gorilla to be), which meant he could hit the ground running and become as gorilla-like as he needed. He closed his eyes and dived in.

He fired the hack packages ahead of him. Worms, disguised as background updates, poured into the surface systems and deadened the security software to Randolph's malicious request for access. The big tech companies promised safety from hacking attacks but, in truth, there was hardly anything individual users could do against a targeted attack. In a handful of milliseconds, the sensory feed and whole body control of his target was routed to him in his hotel suite chair. His own body fell away from him, forgotten, and he inhabited a new skin which was his to control.

His eyes refocused. Immediately he knew something was wrong. He was in some sort of conference room, standing near a large oval table. He looked around the room. Five men sat at the table, although they were currently all looking at something at the back of the room, where a large enclosure with glass walls dominated the rear corner. Inside it was the gorilla, Damba.

Randolph had jumped into the wrong body. How had that happened? Had he been deflected by intrusion countermeasures? Was it something to do with the fuzziness of the new port's data signal?

He felt a sudden nausea, not unusual upon arrival and put a hand on the table to steady himself. It was a slender hand, and there was a silver bangle on the wrist. It looked like a woman's hand. He raised it up and turned it around. He might have been looking at the hand, but his mind was now interrogating the sensory input from across his body. He felt the muscle tension in the woman's legs. He felt the ache in her shoulders and the balls of her feet. He felt the rhythm of her breathing and the beat of her heart. He could feel the stress in her body. He could not yet determine if this was anger or fear or excitement.

The most obvious knee-jerk thing to do right now was to pull out, cancel the hack, return to his body and then attempt to access the gorilla again. But the woman would know something had happened. Even though he would have left no trail, alarms would be raised and the Symbio people would be alerted to a potential hack. That would not be a good thing. He was here now and could not simply back out.

Across the room, behind the men, three women sat in

chairs by the wall. He recognised the learned passivity in
them. Bodyhosts. One of them was looking at him. He
avoided eye contact.

Despite the wilder rumours, bodyhacking did not allow
the hacker access to the target's inner thoughts. Even though
it felt like he was squatting inside her head, he was doing no
such thing. His conscious mind was still very much in his
body, unfelt, on the couch, equally unfelt, beneath him. Her
nerve signals en route to her thalamus were copied and
transmitted via her port to his and, in reply, signals from his
brain, rather than going his own spinal cord, were
transmitted port-to-port down to her central nervous system
motor neurons. At no point was he getting any access to her
brain. To think otherwise was to be as naïve as those early
cinema-goers who ran away at the sight of a train bearing
down on them on screen.

However, this woman was typically lazy, keeping a lot of
information in unencrypted areas of her brain port. Recently
delivered and public data were entirely available to him.
Randolph flicked through it at speed, to give him some
information on what exactly was going on. At the moment,
the five men were generally looking at the gorilla, but sooner
or later he would be expected to do or say something, and he
had no idea what that was supposed to be. He needed to
work through this and plucked at data to fill the gaps. Who
did he recognise in the room? The smug-looking Asian guy
was Krish Sethi, and that bigger guy was Martin Drummond
of Symbio. Therefore, Randolph figured, that probably
meant he was in the body of Constance Wileman, animal
neuroscientist.

The other three men were from the investment firm. Constance's personal assistant flagged them up with handy tags: Dom, Don and Bozza. Randolph had landed right in the middle of the investment pitch meeting. The gorilla was not supposed to be in this room. Randolph's whole plan was now compromised because the gorilla had been re-located.

One of the men, Bozza, from Manticore got up and walked towards the gorilla, hand already raised to tap on the glass.

"Don't rap on the glass," Randolph said. It was important to say something authoritative early on in a meeting, everyone knew that. He might not have any context for what had gone on before he arrived, but this was a no-brainer. He was surprised to hear the voice that came out of him. It was lighter in tone than he was used to, less powerful.

The Manticore man rapped on the glass, not even looking over. Randolph frowned. Damba reacted by rolling to his feet and baring his teeth, clearly detecting a threat, but unsure where it was coming from.

"As I was saying..." said Krish, who had clearly lost track of what he was saying.

"And who do I have to kill round here to get a coffee?" grinned Bozza.

"I believe there's some on the way," said Martin. "Maybe you could go and chase it up, Constance?"

"Me?"

Everyone stared at him, mild confusion on their faces. Why the confusion? He was an animal neuroscientist, not the tea lady. Randolph stumbled as he took a step. High heels. These shoes were ridiculous! He gripped the back of the seat, trying not to look panicked by his inability to walk. He took tiny steps, forcing himself not to look down to see what his feet were doing. "Er, sure," Randolph said.

*No, you're Constance,* he told himself firmly. He had to visualise himself as Constance if he was to succeed.

# 12

Randolph made to leave the room. He needed to do better at this walking thing, conscious of his unnatural staggering. He had ridden along in the bodies of women before, legally. It was one of the things people did when first given the opportunity to body hop: who didn't want to know what it felt like to be the opposite gender? And Randolph had spent enough bored nights alone in foreign hotels to sample almost every available variant of bodysurfing pornography. Oh, he had ridden inside high-heel-wearing women plenty of times but he'd never had to steer one.

He tried to visualise a woman walking. The picture which came into his head was a catwalk model. They did a kind of swaggering, prancing thing, as he recalled. Standing very erect, he swung a leg forward, leading from the hips. He very nearly put a hand to his hip, but decided that it would be too much. He managed three steps before his heel skidded out from underneath him and he stumbled again. He caught himself on the back of another chair. Faces turned to look at him. He would have no credibility with this group left at all. He strode forward again and this time he made it out of the room without incident. He leant against a nearby wall and removed the shoes. He padded in stockinged feet to the end of the corridor. There was a man in a waistcoat pushing a trolley.

"Hey! Is there some coffee on the way to this meeting room?" Randolph called.

"Yes, madam. It will be there in one moment."

With that taken care of, he had a moment to decide what to do. He could jump out of the woman's body now and try to hijack the ape regardless. He still didn't like his chances. He could walk her round to Spike's van at the rear of the hotel, get Spike to tie her up and hold her hostage until the job was done. But he couldn't think of a way of doing that without Constance getting a good look at Spike, or picking up incriminating details during the conversation.

Randolph needed some way to get Constance out of the way so he could do his job properly. He walked through hotel reception as he thought on this and recognised that he'd already decided what he had to do. He stepped outside, from air-conditioned hotel to baking sunshine, and walked along the paved driveway towards the dual-carriage highway. There was no one around.

"So," he said out loud, "I think you're in there somewhere, Constance, and, as best as I understand it, can see all of this. Like a ride-along movie show."

The gravel-flecked path pinched at the exposed soles of his feet.

"I'm really a nice person," he said. "Honestly. Strong moral compass. If you met me in real life, you'd like me. But I've got a job to do and I've dropped into the wrong body. I just need to get you out of the way for a while."

There was a short slip road from the park resort to the highway. Driverless freight vehicles zipped along at speed in an intermittent stream.

"This is going to hurt. I can't deny it," he said. "But I'm not going to kill you, okay? I'm not going to abuse my position. I want to do the right thing. But this is going to hurt."

He reached the end of the slip road and stood at the highway's edge. They were on an elevated strip of land and, across the busy highway, he could see the towers of the city and the sparkling blue sea beyond. He looked at the speeding traffic. He just needed to find the right vehicle. He needed an impact hard enough to break a leg, maybe give mild concussion. That was all.

"Don't think about what's about to happen," he said. "Think about the positives. It's a sunny day. There's a nice breeze ... somewhere. It's a beautiful city. There's a lot of beauty around you. Don't think about what's about to happen."

Randolph watched the traffic. The freight vehicles, rectangular boxes of hardened plastic and steel, flashed by, every single one of them moving at the seventy kilometres per hour speed limit. It would be hard to get hit by one of them without becoming instant road pancake.

Randolph put out a hand experimentally. The vehicle beeped automatically but did not slow.

"It's only going to hurt a little," he said.

He looked at his feet – Constance's feet. All he had to do was step out into traffic and he would be free to do the job properly. It was all he had to do.

He looked up at the truck approaching in the nearside lane.

## 13

Randolph, still very much in Constance's body, locked himself into a toilet cubicle in the hotel lobby. He hadn't done it. He couldn't do it. He couldn't distinguish between moral squeamishness and the rational fear that he might be arrested for causing the woman serious harm but, whatever the case, he had not been able to walk her into traffic.

For better or worse, he was stuck with this woman for the duration.

He sat on the closed toilet seat. "What am I going to do?" he said out loud and sighed.

His options seemed to have come down to give up and leave, or press on in her body.

He would have to try something radical. He was a skilled puppeteer and could alter which systems of her body he controlled at will. He opened a text window in her brain port and allowed her access to that file and that file alone.

*Hi Constance,* he typed in the file.

Her response was instantaneous. *Control command: reboot systems. Control command: reboot systems.*

He would have tried the same thing, if he were her. *Hey Constance. You know that won't work. This is just a text field. We need to chat.*

*You need to get the hell out of my brain! You tried to fucking kill me.*

Randolph blinked. *I did not try to kill you. I specifically did not kill you. You saw quite clearly that I did not kill you when I quite clearly could have.*

*Fuck off! You need to get out of my head now. This is a first degree data assault.*

*In some countries, yes. Here, I believe the law is a bit more woolly.*

*Who are you and what are you doing?*

*You can call me Derek. I make my living brokering intellectual property.*

There was a pause. She was thinking it over. She was thinking, on the plus side, this wasn't some random crazy in his head, not some mind-rapist attacker. She was thinking, on the negative side, she was dealing with a professional, someone undoubtedly smarter than her. *What do you want?*

*The gorilla.*

*You have taken over my brain and you plan to steal our products. Why would I talk to you?*

*Because you don't really have an alternative.*

It was a weak play and Randolph knew it. He couldn't rely on Constance being so bored or lonely she would chat to him just for fun. He needed something better than that.

*Let me put it this way, Constance. I can't just leave at this point and think up another way to get the gorilla, can I? So, I'm stuck in here until I can find a way to get the gorilla out of—*

*—Damba.*

*Fine. Until I can get Damba out of here. Now the way I see it is this. You and I both know things are moving pretty quickly in this industry. I reckon Symbio is about four months ahead of the competition. Four months. That means if I hang around in your head for that long, stalling your investment plans, then your company's innovation has lost its value anyway.*

There was silence. Randolph could imagine Constance weighing up the horror of being a passenger in her own body for four months versus the humiliation of helping him.

*What do you want from me?*

Randolph smiled. *Just a few small details, so that I can get a plan B underway. Let's start with those three from Manticore. What do you know about them?*

*Nothing at all. Bozza is the lead, but I never met them before.*

*Huh. I assumed there was some history there. He gave me an odd look, well, not a look at all.*

*What? When?*

*Why did they ignore me when I told them not to rap on the glass?*

There was a pause. Randolph congratulated himself for his observation skills, obviously there was indeed some history there.

*You'll have noticed by now, Derek – if that is your real name—*

*Of course it isn't.*

*—You'll have noticed that you're in the body of a woman,*

*right? By the way, if you touch this body in any way that I do not approve of, then you can absolutely fuck yourself for four solid months, because my help will be immediately withdrawn. Understood?*

*Understood. Seriously I'm a stand up guy. I respect women.*

*Fucker. Like I said, you are in the body of a woman. There is a good chance that you will be ignored and interrupted.*

In the flesh, Randolph tutted and glanced to the ceiling. *Hah! I've heard this before. You're going to tell me that men ignore you because you're a woman?*

*Yes.*

*I hate to break it to you, but it'll be down to the way you talk.*

*The way I talk?*

*Men have no patience for small talk, or indecision. Especially ones with important jobs, where time is in short supply.*

*There isn't an emoji in this text format for screaming so you'll have to pretend that I'm screaming. You think [you absolute fucking moron] that men ignore me because I'm making small talk?*

*I'm saying it's the WAY you talk that is counter-productive in business situations. Shouldn't be a problem for me, I've dealt with power brokers.*

*Right. Sure. Do you happen to know what percentage of venture capitalists are men?*

*What's that got to do with anything?*

*Do you know the percentage?*

*Er, no. Why would I know a thing like that? Fifty per cent?*

*Ninety three per cent. So basically, that industry is ENTIRELY male. The culture in an industry like that does not favour women.*

*No, you've misunderstood. This is not the twentieth century. Everyone knows that the playing field has been level for years. Women could be part of that world if they wanted to but they're much happier—*

*Making small talk?*

*Watch and learn. Don't blame your gender for being ignored in the boardroom. You wait until you see me in action.*

*You're a real prize, Derek. You're actually suggesting that I've been womanning all wrong, and what I really needed was a man to show me how to do it?*

He couldn't blame her for being hostile. He had very nearly walked her in front of a truck.

*No, that isn't what I mean. I just know that purposeful business communication doesn't come naturally to a woman. Putting your point across, knowing exactly when to interrupt someone else's conversational flow. It's an art and it's a dirty one. Maybe you're nicer people or something. Regardless, I need to get Damba out of there and we're going to do it in this body. What's the schedule for the day?*

*I have no idea. Krish was the one who changed things around to put him in the room with us. You'd need to get those details off him.*

*Right. You get on well with him, though? He'll share that if I ask?*

*Yes, he will.*

Randolph was back in business! He was starting to see a way forward. He would go back to the meeting, make sure everyone was happy (but not so happy that they wrapped up any deals fast enough for Damba to disappear off site) and then intercept Damba as he was being removed later on. He grinned to himself and put a hand on the lock of the door.

# 14

Randolph made his way back to the meeting room, electing to leave the high heels off.

Martin and the investment lads were sipping coffee in the meeting room, so he poured himself a cup and sat down. Krish was finishing off a presentation with similar content to the video that Randolph had watched, although there was a lot more detail regarding projected growth and market share.

"You know what?" Bozza said. "Our due diligence people have been through this. The figures all check out, and we're happy that the projections line up with our tier one."

"Tier one?" Krish asked.

"That's the lowest of the tiers we model for return on investment. You should know we rarely invest in projects below a tier three."

There was a pause. Randolph ported a question about

the day's schedule to Krish and then made the obvious and necessary observation to the investors. "And yet you're here."

Bozza smiled broadly. "Yes, we are! That's because we've spotted an alternative revenue stream that outperforms this one by a country mile. If it helps to move things along I can share some details with you. What do you think? I'm being as transparent as I can with you. I'm sure we all recognise the value of that. We're all busy people, yeah?"

Krish glanced over at Martin. "Sure," said Martin.

Randolph looked at him carefully. Martin might be the boss, but he was looking a little flustered. They were on the back foot, and Bozza knew it, grinning like a smug bastard. Bozza ported a set of slide images at them all and started to talk through them.

"So, we approached this from a different angle. What you're really selling here is a remote controlled gorilla, and who doesn't need one of those?" His grin amplified as he looked around the room. "We think there are lots of buyers out there for your boy Damba, and they'll pay more than the eco-warriors. A *lot* more." He pointed at the cage where Damba sat cross-legged on the floor, pulling at his toes in a lacklustre display of what appeared to be extreme boredom. "We looked at a range of customer archetypes and there are several with good potential. There's the bored playboy who wants to get his kicks swinging through the jungle, although he doesn't know it yet. He'll pay big bucks for the chance to feel that strength and agility. However, we see an outsized risk in that those same customers might get litigious if they find part of the experience unsavoury, whether it's grooming for fleas or flinging poop or whatever."

"That sort of behaviour tends to be associated with captive apes," said Krish. Randolph couldn't read his face. Was he quietly aghast or secretly admiring this bold departure?

"Interesting. Still, the point holds," said Bozza. "So we looked at the mining industry in the Congo."

*Fuck*, typed Constance.

"As you know," said Bozza, "some of the products from artisanal mines are crucial to the tech world, so the rewards can be huge. We estimate that a gorilla would out-perform a human worker by two hundred and fifty per cent in what's known to be an intensely physical job. Again though, we must consider the risks, and the world's eyes are on these mines now, much more so than in the past. A public backlash could destroy this model entirely." Bozza made sure everyone's eyes were on him. "Which brings me to the third option. These particular customers will be willing to spend the money, and there are a lot of them." He shuffled the slide image forward. "The militia groups of central Africa."

The slide showed a familiar-looking scene of soldiers in camouflage fatigues, piling off the back of an ancient Toyota Hilux. The thing which arrested the eye was the gorilla that had been photoshopped into the centre of the scene, holding an M16. Randolph had to work hard to suppress a grin: the gorilla was the most badass sight imaginable. He glanced over at Krish and Martin. They were both awestruck. Bozza left the image hanging for a long moment without comment, knowing its raw appeal did all the talking. When he eventually moved onto another slide, it was graphs of sales projections. They showed the comparison between Symbio's original proposal and this new version. Krish and Martin made noises of muted appreciation at the opportunities.

*Speak up*, typed Constance. *You can't allow this.*

*Allow it?* Randolph replied. *You were offering the world remote controlled gorillas and didn't think it would go this way? Even I could have predicted that.*

*Object! Object now. You can do it because it's morally wrong or you can do it because it will keep them in the room longer.*

"Hey, you guys," said Randolph. "You know when something looks too good to be true, it probably is?"

Nobody acknowledged him.

"The figures speak for themselves," said Bozza. "If you truly want Symbio to play on the world stage then this is the way to go."

"There are some serious challenges—" Randolph started.

"—It looks fantastic!" said Martin.

"I agree," breathed Krish. "This takes things to another level."

Randolph needed to insert himself into the discussion. Constance was right. He could not afford to let the deal get wrapped up so quickly, in case Damba was taken away prematurely. What was bizarre, though was that any fool could see that there were some serious flaws in this strategy.

Bozza was holding court again, talking through numbers. "Even being pessimistic about the take-up of this offer I think we can see that—"

"What about the challenges—?" Randolph started.

Bozza looked over at him with a frown of admonishment and continued to talk. "—I think we can see that the projections are as solid as they possibly can be."

What was that all about? Randolph was incredulous. Bozza wasn't even saying anything new! He was circling round on the same self-congratulatory story. Was he so self-centred he simply couldn't bear to be interrupted? Randolph waited for an opportunity to speak. On the third attempt he managed to finish a sentence.

"There are some significant challenges here," he said, raising his voice so that nobody could fail to hear.

"Oh?" said Bozza. "Well, I'm sure we can look at those for you. By the way, is there some more coffee coming?"

"What?" Randolph growled. He raised himself up to his full height, but then remembered that Constance's height was around five three instead of his usual six one.

Everyone turned to stare.

"Would you *please* listen to me!" he said loudly.

"Whoa, Constance. What's got into you?" Martin said, his face concerned. "I understand you might get a little emotional about our plans changing so rapidly, but maybe you want to take a moment, yeah? Go see if you can rustle up some more coffee and we'll talk when you come back."

He gave a friendly, supportive smile, but the room paused, waiting for Randolph to leave.

# 15

Randolph padded out to the corridor, noticing on the way how heavy the conference room door was for his female arms. It was one of those that stretched from floor to ceiling, which was a fine choice for style, but why on earth did he have to lean against it to open it, making him look feeble?

Around the corner he found a seat. *What the hell just happened?* he typed.

*Holy shit, Derek,* Constance replied. *What do you want me to start with? The dick weasels who want to deploy ape soldiers into the African Congo? The limited vision of Krish and Martin once the dollar signs appear in their eyes? No, let's start with you apologising to me about not taking my word for how women are treated in meetings like this. Go on, I'm waiting.*

*Jesus. Break it down for me. What just happened?*

*Hey, get over yourself. I don't have the time or the knowledge to do the whole 'In the beginning there was the Patriarchy' thing.*

*You got treated like a woman and you didn't like it. Boo-fucking-hoo. We need to move on and we need to be a whole lot smarter about how we do it, or Damba and all of the other great apes are screwed.*

*Hey, I tried! They wouldn't listen!*

*Enough! I can tell you how to get a point across, but you need to strap in and pay attention or we'll be out of time.*

*Out of time?*

*Watch out for them slapping each other on the back when you go back in. They'll be forming a little male clique and you won't be able to get inside it. You need to sort out that coffee and you need to go round and see how everybody likes it while you top them up. You need to make them like you again.*

*Seriously?*

*We're into damage limitation now. Then, as you're moving around the room, and everyone's relaxed and chatty, you need to say something like 'Hey guys, I have a dumb question' and someone will smile indulgently and say 'There's no such thing as a dumb question' and then you ask whether they have thought about the growing interest in great apes being assigned personhood, and, ohh, isn't that a massive risk to an idea like this?*

*So, I have to grovel for airtime?*

*Yes, you do. You need to appear non-threatening. They will give you some bullshit answer, but your main task here is to turn Martin's head. Try saying that his husband, Graham, will not approve. Graham works as a veterinarian, and I can say without a doubt he will have some strong opinions on this. Bring them to the forefront of his mind.*

*What about Krish?*

*He will only care about the PR disaster this could bring. The trouble we have there is that rogue militia are not like companies trading on the stock exchange. Nobody's going to post negative reviews on the internet or arrange a boycott. It's a covert world and that works in their favour. Mind you, Krish is a yes-man and very much a coward. If you can spot an opportunity to seed the idea that some terrifying warlord will visit him in the middle of the night to punish him for his part in it, then that could work.*

*Right. Coffee, grovelling and subtle mind games. Got it.*

*Welcome to my world.*

Randolph composed the most serene expression he could muster as he wheeled the coffee trolley into the room. The men were clustered around a table, chatting.

"Ah, coffee!" Bozza said. He slapped Martin and Krish on the shoulder as he walked back to get his cup.

*Back-slapping ahoy*, said Constance.

Randolph bristled. Didn't they all see what a snub it was for him to be omitted from this masculine display?

"Milk and sugar?" he asked each of them in turn as he served them with a friendly smile. "Oh, hey, I have a question for you. It's probably a dumb one."

"Relax," said Bozza. "This is a safe space. Besides, there are no dumb questions. What do you want to know?"

"I was thinking about how some animals have been granted human rights by countries in recent years. Great apes, cetaceans, that super-intelligent octopus in Greece. If that trend continues, won't it threaten this business model you're proposing?"

Bozza nodded as if he were agreeing. "I'm so glad you called it out as a *trend*, Constance," he said, "because that's very much what it is. A bandwagon which a few environmental extremists have jumped on in a few countries. I think we're fairly well insulated from that kind of radicalism in the markets we're entering here."

Randolph had to hand it to him for some quick-thinking weasel-wordery. He could see Martin nodding with relief from the corner of his eye. "Oh that's good news," Randolph said with a pleasant smile. He turned to Martin. "Maybe you could get Graham's input? He must be very well-versed in which way things are going. More coffee?"

"Graham?" said Bozza. Randolph saw Martin's face fall as he considered what his vet husband's thoughts might be.

Bozza saw it too, and he moved across the room with his arms raised, as if in anticipation of an embrace. "Men of vision must often allay the doubts of those around them. I have every confidence that you're capable Martin. Every confidence."

Martin straightened and gave a nod of acknowledgement.

Randolph concentrated as hard as he could on appearing non-threatening, when all he wanted to do was bang heads together and yell at these idiots for being such naive pushovers. He tilted his head and smiled. He even gave a sharp clap of his hands. Too much? Apparently not. "Oh yes. Martin is very capable, which is why we all look up to him. Would I be right in thinking that the world of the military is a little different from the world of business, Bozza? I guess Krish needs to understand how to conduct himself when he runs a sales campaign. How would he protect himself from these people? Some of them sound quite dangerous."

Randolph willed Krish to pick up on the hint of danger. Yes! There it was. The nervous sideways glance.

"Um, yeah, how would we make sales?" asked Krish.

"Oh mate!" Another shoulder slap. "Nothing to worry about, seriously. We'll have a stand at the biggest of the trade fairs and the orders will come rolling in."

"Arms fairs?" Randolph said.

Bozza gave a dismissive nod. "Trade fairs." He sidled closer to Krish. "Those things are a hoot. The tales I could tell! Maybe I will tell you if we have a beer or three later, whaddya say?"

Krish smiled and Randolph knew his attempt had failed. He took a seat and sipped coffee. *Any more ideas Constance?*

*You've lost, surely you can see that? Why don't you get out of my brain now? It's over.*

*No can do. That ape needs to come with me.*

*You won't get away with it.*

*So, you're just going to let Damba become a soldier. Is that what you want, Constance?*

*Of course I don't you fool! But if I'm going to suffer I don't see why I should do it as a passenger in my own head, do you?*

*You haven't heard my Plan B yet.*

*I'm all ears.*

Randolph stewed in his seat, his small womanly hands around his coffee cup and wondered what Plan B might be.

## 16

On the third time of asking, Krish ported an itinerary for the day to Randolph/Constance.

*Beers at Granada. What's this?* he immediately messaged back.

*Bozza suggested it,* replied Krish. *Didn't think you'd be up for it.*

*And welcome to being a woman in a man's world,* said Constance in the text field.

Randolph smiled. This was great. The men were off out for some self-congratulatory beers and he wasn't invited.

The bodyhost women were first to leave the room. Randolph even saw the shake the young woman gave as her host departed.

"Beer o'clock," said Dom the investor, standing.

Martin gathered his table stationery as he stood. "Constance ... I didn't know if you wanted to..." He didn't look like he was going to finish the sentence.

*He's expecting you to say you don't want to join them*, said Constance.

*Won't it seem odd if I decline?*

*It would be odder if you insisted on going.*

"I might join you later," said Randolph. "You boys have fun."

There was visible relief on Martin's face which was just the weirdest reaction.

Randolph turned to Krish. "What about Damba? Is he being cared for?"

"Of course, the team will be up for him at five and he'll go back to the environment next door. He'll be fine."

"Great!"

Apart from Martin, the men didn't even look back when they left. Randolph checked local information. Granada was a mall about three kilometres away with a bar that served alcohol. Three kilometres was a good distance.

*Still don't think men treat women differently?* said Constance.

Randolph jerked a thumb at the closed door. "They just want to go off and do bloke stuff. I'm sure you and your female colleagues might want to do girly stuff some times."

*Me and my female colleagues? Take a look around you. I'm not going to ask you what girly stuff you think that might be.*

Randolph approached Damba's glass-sided cage and checked the time. "We've got an hour before they come to take him back to his enclosure. Probably at least another hour before the boys even think about coming back. That's plenty of time to get Damba into the van and away."

*You think it's as simple as that.*

"I think you and I want the same thing," said Randolph. "I want Damba and you want to stop Damba being a monkey soldier."

*He's not a monkey, he's an ape. Also, those two goals are not quite the same thing. Manticore want to turn him and his species into soldier slaves. Your employer or client or whatever probably wants something similar.*

Randolph laughed. "Definitely not. If you knew my employer..."

*Yeah? Well, I don't.*

"What do you want then?"

Constance was silent. Randolph poured himself another coffee. The pot was still warm enough.

*I want to cancel the sale to Manticore.*

"Okay."

*I want to put a halt to everything until I've done some high-kinetic cranial cognition therapy on my colleagues.*

"Huh?"

*I'm going to bash their heads together until I've knocked some sense into them. And I want Damba to go back to the wild, unmolested.*

"With a multi-million dollar brain port in his head?"

*I have a plan,* she typed.

"Hey, I'm the plans guy. You're just the body I'm driving."

*Or, how about you listen to my plan and then go 'gosh, Constance, that's a swell plan. I wish I'd listened to you in the first place'?*

Randolph humphed. "Lay it on me, sister."

*Damba won't be safe from either you or Manticore while he still has the Symbio port in his head.*

"I'm not sure that's the wording I'd use…"

*We have a master control device here at the hotel.*

"What kind of a master control device?"

There was a noise at the door. Randolph whirled, but it was just one of the hotel staff with a covered trolley come to take away the coffee things. Randolph gestured for them to get on with it and returned to his conversation. No way of them knowing he wasn't on an audio call to colleagues elsewhere.

"What kind of device?"

*It can track the brain port. It can be used to deliver a crippling neuro-shock to Damba, a necessary evil if you're transporting a four hundred pound gorilla. And there's a grey goo auto-destruct command.*

"Auto-destruct?"

*Turns the port nanos into harmless grey nano-goo in case – oh, I don't know – some prick tries to kidnap our gorilla.*

"Ah."

*We should get the device and use it to destroy Damba's brain port.*

"That's the very prize I came for."

*True, but in return I will connect to Symbio's secure data site and download the brain port schematics for you.*

Randolph considered the offer and a second later, brought up a network access window in Constance's vision. "Access details and passwords," he said.

*No deal. I'm not laying bare all Symbio's files and secrets for you. My colleagues may be weak-willed pillocks, but they're still my colleagues, and it's still my company. Give me access to my own port. Private access.*

"I don't know if I can trust you."

*Says the man who is literally in control of my entire body.*

That much was true, but if she could port out to Symbio there were things she could do. But what? Send an e-mail? Post a cry for help? Such things were possible, but even if she did, what real-world impact would it have on Randolph?

"You've got thirty seconds to download the schematics to this port or I take this body outside and walk it in front of a bus," he said.

*So charming. So trusting*, she replied.

He flexed and granted brain port access to her. He watched the data stats as she reached out across the internet.

# 17

Constance had decided one of them was very stupid. She hoped it was Randolph.

The plan she had detailed to her hijacker was one she could quite happily have gone through with. She and Martin had set up the company to further neuro-data technology, but also to have a genuine impact on animal welfare and wild populations. If Martin was going to sell out to amoral investors and their warlord chums, she'd happily wipe out the brain port data files. Of course, it wouldn't stop Martin rebuilding and reconstructing, but it would set Symbio back months, and give him time to reflect on what an utter twat he was capable of being.

Constance could have quite happily (and quite spitefully) gone through with that plan, but Randolph, unthinking, had given her a doorway out and access to her own brain port.

She opened up access to Symbio's data site but went no

further. Instead, she looked back at her port and the traffic moving through it. The simple functioning of the human brain required a data transfer rate of approximately eleven megabits per second, a drop in the ocean for a modern brain port. Managing the flow of sensory data in one direction and control instructions in the other, all packaged in such a way that her hijacker had seamless control over her, required considerably more bandwidth. The flow of data between her and the bodyhacker was easily identified. Looking at it from the outside, as it were, the protocols by which he had brute-forced his way into her body were transparent.

"Twenty seconds," she heard her own voice say.

All she had to do was latch onto the sensory data going out and add her own control protocols. Had this arrogant man forgotten that she was a brain scientist?

Constance grabbed, tagged, twisted and edited the data stream.

...

SHE OPENED HER EYES.

There was a pale ceiling and a light shade of concentric yellow cylinders above her. The body was lying on a soft couch and, when she sat up, her whole body ached at once. There was a painless but unpleasant tugging at her crotch. She blinked to focus her eyes.

A catheter snaked up from a urine pouch to her penis. She had a penis. It had worked.

Constance sat still for several minutes. It was unusual to be in control of another body. She had ridden in other human hosts before, and her job had entailed taking control of laboratory monkeys and apes like Damba. But it didn't come easy. A new body had a new gait. Muscles developed or atrophied in response to the habits of the previous owner. Like an old manual car, where the sponginess of the brakes or the truculence of the gearbox varied from vehicle to vehicle, so too varied the control mechanisms of individual human bodies.

She stood slowly, shook out one tired leg, then the other. "Well, the boot is on the other foot now, eh?" she said, laughing at the aptness of the saying.

She had a deeper voice. Not a surprise, but the way it rumbled in her throat, like she had a permanent throat infection, was a novel sensation.

The weight of the catheter bag tugged at her as she moved. She felt a momentary revulsion at touching a bag part-filled with someone else's urine. Reasoning to herself that if she touched it, it would be with someone else's hands, not hers, she picked it up and tucked it down the front of her trousers.

She moved to the room telephone, an antiquated touch in this posh hotel, and picked up the receiver. "Could you put me through to the local police please?"

She opened a text window, as her hijacker had done for her. This moment of revenge was too sweet to be enjoyed alone.

*Wait. Stop. Don't do this*, he typed.

"Don't do what, you utter prick?" she growled. "You invaded my body and tried to steal my life's work! How dare you? How *dare* you?"

*Hey. We had a deal.*

"Oh sorry, officer." The officer on the line had spoken in something other than English but the brain port had offered an instant translation. "Yes, I would like to report a crime."

*Do not do this. It will not end well.*

The egotistical arsehole was still trying act like he had the upper hand.

"Yes, I would like to turn myself in," she said to the police officer. "I'm guilty of acts of bodyhacking and industrial espionage. That's right. Me." She looked around for a coat or a wallet or similar. There was a light jacket on the bed.

*Do not do this. It's not helping Damba.*

She felt in the jacket pockets and found a physical passport. There were so few forms of physical ID these days, but a passport was still required for some countries.

"Yes, my name ... is *not* Derek. Lying bastard. It's Randolph Howard. I'm at the Al Bahyah Park Resort Hotel, room..."

*Fuck fuck fuck fuck fuck*, Randolph typed. Each little word was a thrill of pleasure to Constance.

She walked to the French windows and stepped out onto the balcony. She looked down. The zoological gardens, a blast of green between the sea and the desert, was a long way below.

"I'm on at least the tenth floor," she said to the police

officer. "It's hard to count. You could check with reception when you come to arrest me."

She let the phone drop to the floor. She looked at the ground far below and wondered how long it would take a falling object to hit it.

"You were going to walk my body into traffic," she said, leaning out over the balcony. Even though this wasn't her body, and the event of his death would have no physical impact on her, she instinctively held back from leaning too far. She fought the instinct and eased his entire upper body over the rail so that it balanced, almost perfectly, capable of tilting one way or the other.

*Please*, he typed.

"Pleading with me now."

*It was just a job. And I'm sorry. It's not as if I enjoyed it or anything.*

"That is not the point, you ignorant twat."

*You've got every right to be angry, Constance. What I did was unforgiveable, but please don't kill me. I really do have a plan to save Damba.*

She laughed at that. "I don't need you. I'm the one with the plan."

She pushed back from the balcony edge and returned to the hotel suite. They probably had at least ten minutes, more if the police thought it was a hoax call, which was likely. And she had no idea how responsive the local police were anyway.

She headed out onto the corridor and called the lift. She saw they were actually on the twelfth floor and momentarily considered calling the police again. She took the lift down to the fifth floor where she, Martin and Krish had their more modest rooms.

"The master control device is in Krish's room," she informed Randolph as she walked. "It's a company booking, so I should have access to his room."

She ported the door to his room to open. It didn't respond. She ported it again. Still nothing.

"Why's it not working?"

… … … … … … … A string of ellipses appeared in the text field.

"Is that you sulking silently? Or just being quietly smug?" she said before realising. She was riding Randolph's body. It was his brain port she was using and he didn't have access. It was like trying to open an old-fashioned door with the wrong thumbprint.

"I need my body," she said.

*Or I could hack the lock for you*, said Randolph.

"No, thank you," she said. "I can do this myself."

*But you can't.*

"I can just wait until the police take you away, return to my own body, then access it properly."

*Fine. Go. Leave me now.*

"Wait? Give control back to you? And open myself up to a fresh hacking attempt? I'll wait for the cops."

*Could be a while.*

"You and I are not on the same team, Randolph. I'm not giving you the schematics anymore."

*But neither of us want the Manticore guys to have Damba.*

That was true enough. "Fine. Tell me how to hack the door."

*I can't tell you how to perform a skill. There's nuance. There's an art to it.*

She smirked. "Sure. Whatever." She sighed. "Okay. I'm opening up limited access to your port so you can—"

She felt a rush, a blinding force of data, and the mental cybernetic equivalent of a judo flip.

## 18

Randolph picked himself up off the meeting room floor.

The hotel staff who had crowded round Constance's comatose body, fanning him with their tea towels, stepped back and helped him up.

"I'm okay," he assured them, smoothing down his blouse. "Just fainted from the heat."

*Fucking fucking fucker*, said Constance in the text field.

Randolph smiled with Constance's lips and gently urged the people away. "I just need to get back to my room," he said.

What he needed to do, of course, was get to the fifth floor and reclaim his own, now comatose body.

"This was supposed to be a simple job," he muttered under his breath.

*You're a thief, a crook and a liar*, Constance typed.

"And you told the police my real name."

His identity was out in the open. The value of secrecy was almost entirely eroded. Once he had his own body safely gathered there was nothing to stop him walking Constance to the van and getting Spike to tie Constance up so he, Randolph, could get on with his originally planned job. He just had to—

He stopped, stock still, in reception. His own limp body was being carried out, a police officer supporting an arm each over their necks, as though were carrying a drunk friend home.

"Balls," he said.

Constance gave him a smiley emoji.

"This is not good," he said and followed the police out. There was an armoured van parked up in front of the hotel. A senior, moustachioed officer was talking in urgent tones with a suited member of hotel staff. The conversation was irritable and not good-natured, but Randolph really didn't care to listen in. His eyes were only on his body being put into the back of the van.

This was an out of body experience of the very worst kind. He did not want to return to his own body just so he could discover what local prisons were like.

"Wait!" he said.

*What are you doing?* said Constance.

The police officers had dumped Randolph's body on the van floor. "What?" said one.

"Doesn't he need an ambulance?" said Randolph.

The senior officer had torn himself away from the hotel concierge. "You know this man?"

"No. But he looks ill. I think he needs medical attention."

"Go back inside. We will take care of him."

"You need to call an ambulance."

The officer's contempt was grossly apparent. "You need to move away or we will arrest you too."

The nearest officer had his pistol in his holster, unsecured. Randolph could step forward and take it. If they thought she was just a pathetic woman, they wouldn't be expecting such a manoeuvre.

*Do not get me arrested too*, said Constance.

The officer with the unsecured pistol caught her gaze and frowned. Randolph raised his hands to ward him off.

"You know this man!" the officer challenged him.

"No. I've never—"

Randolph leapt, from Constance's body back into his own.

Sensation flooded into his own body, with something akin to pins and needles. Normally, the return was a pleasure – as nice as it was to travel, it was always good to come home – but he had no time to appreciate that now. He rolled over on the floor of the van.

Constance was gasping, on the verge of screaming.

Randolph propelled himself forward and tried to grab the policeman's gun. He didn't see the other officer swing round and punch him in the neck, then slam the door in his face. He had a split second to wish Constance was on board to share the pain before he blacked out.

# 19

Constance looked at Randolph. Randolph looked at Constance.

They were both in their own bodies, both sitting in the back of the police van, and both handcuffed.

As best as Constance could work out there was at least one of the policeman in the cab behind the metal grille, but the van was still stationary outside the hotel. The other two officers had perhaps gone into the hotel. To search Randolph's room for evidence? To gather clues as to what the hell was going on?

"I'd like to say I'm ... sorry," said Randolph.

Constance stared at him, this handsome long streak of piss in his expensive suit trousers and crisp white shirt. "What do you want?" she said.

He blinked. "Really. Just to say sorry. I didn't want it to end like this for you, stuck in the back of hot police van – it's getting hotter in here, isn't it? – and getting arrested."

She wanted to give him a superior smile, but she wasn't feeling very superior at the moment. "I'll be out in no time," she said. "I've done nothing wrong. I will tell them the truth."

"Yes, but—"

"Whereas you are going to jail and will have a very nasty time of it."

"I doubt that," he said. "But I appreciate the sentiment."

"You bodyhacked me. Your brain port is full of illegal software."

He shrugged. "I did a total wipe and factory reset on the port the moment they grabbed me, just in case they tried to mirror copy my port state when they arrested me. The police in Switzerland – the only other time I have been arrested – carry these port freezer things. Knock you completely off-grid. It's like a taser for your brain— What are you smiling at?"

She realised the superior smile had come to her naturally after all. "I wondered why you weren't just messaging your little friend for back up or – oh, I don't know – trying to hack Damba from here and getting him to come and rescue you."

He snorted. "Get him to rescue me? He's a gorilla."

"He's a four-hundred pound gorilla. He'd make short work of those doors."

"That's a crazy plan."

"But you wiped your port anyway."

She could see him trying to hold off an expression of bitterness. His face contorted like a cat licking a lemon.

He was right about one thing. It was getting hotter in here. The Middle Eastern sun was beating down on the steel box of the van, and it appeared the local police didn't feel prisoners needed air conditioning.

She received a port notification. It was a message from Krish. It was audio but he hadn't tried to actually call her. Something to share with her which he didn't want to discuss. It was probably just some sappy false sentiment, like it was a shame she couldn't join the lads for some beers. She listened to it anyway.

She listened to it again. "Oh, hell," she sighed.

"What is it?" said Randolph.

She didn't reply at first. She needed to think through all the possibilities and permutations. "Something bad has happened," she said.

"Like I said, I'm sorry."

She shook her hand. "Martin has agreed a deal with the Manticore investors."

"You knew that was going to happen."

"Like a deal, right now. The Manticore guys have chartered a plane. They're taking Damba to a facility they own in South Africa."

"Ah."

She looked around her. "It shouldn't take too long to get things sorted out at the police station. I could get the master control device, get down to the airport and…"

"I suspect the wheels of local justice turn very slowly indeed," said Randolph. "We're both going to be enjoying hot little prison cells until tomorrow, at the earliest."

Constance banged her feet on the metal floor. "Come on! Let's go! I've got places to be!"

Randolph grinned, then sighed. "I am intrigued by your

suggestion of getting Damba to rescue us. He's in range, right?"

"That was just a silly, off the cuff remark. We couldn't..."

She tried to picture it. With a human controller, Damba could break out of his enclosure, true. Go into the hotel, get the master control device, then use it on himself to melt his brain port. All from the back of the van.

"I could," said Constance and reached out.

She had ridden with Damba so many times it was like putting on a familiar coat, a heavy, bulky coat that restricted and changed the way she moved, but a familiar coat nonetheless. She squatted at the back of his mind, taking in sensory input but not seizing control. She – Damba – was sitting in his enclosure in the park zoo. The staff had come in and moved him already. The earth floor beneath him was warm and uneven. Ahead of him were the pieces of artfully constructed tree furniture: trunks to climb, foliage to paw through, ready-made nests to sleep in. Constance could sense a discomfort in Damba's body tension, in his heart rate and nervous energy. He was not having a happy day.

There were hunks of fruit and a selection of leaves in front of him, but he hadn't touched them. He just stroked his belly fur and huffed.

Constance edged forward and took control. She turned Damba's head and looked to the enclosure door. She could do this. Again, she tried to picture herself: controlling Damba, breaking out of the zoo, breaking into the adjacent hotel...

She backed away and into her own body. She let out a worried sigh. "I can't do it."

"Technical issues?" said Randolph.

"Moral issues."

"Really? You don't think saving Damba from a Manticore lab and the field of battle is the right thing to do?"

"I mean I don't know if *I* can do. I'm a scientist. I don't do this super-spy shit like you."

"No one's ever called me a super-spy before."

"Well, whatever."

"I had a girlfriend in Holland who called me a dirty brain-burglar. But that was because I hitched a ride in her head while she was cheating on me with the guy from the corner bookstore."

"You see? You have no morals."

Randolph nodded. "I get it. You need my help after all."

"I didn't say that."

"Since I've wiped my port, you can grant me access to yours. I'll steer Damba out of there, get the master control and, in return, you give me the port schematics. Which was what you had originally promised, I might point out."

It automatically sounded like a bad idea. The man couldn't be trusted. And yet ... she didn't have the power of her own convictions to go through with it alone.

"Open up your port to me," she said. "Give me total access."

"What?"

"Give it to me and I will let you ride along with me."

"But total control..."

"I can't trust you otherwise."

"No way. I don't need you."

"But you need the schematics. Or are you going to tell

your employer that you turned down your only chance of getting them?"

He pulled a miserable, tortured expression. Constance could have watched it all day.

"Fine," he grumped.

"Fine?"

"Let's do this. Before the police actually drive us out of range."

## 20

Randolph pushed the metaphorical button and was inside the gorilla's head.

It was a disconcerting experience to be a passenger inside another head with zero control. He realised immediately why Constance had been so angry: it was the sort of thing that could induce severe panic. He tried to slow his breathing, before admitting even that was beyond his control.

Damba was breathing in ragged huffs. At a guess, the gorilla hadn't had a great day either.

*Where are we?* Randolph typed in the text field Constance had opened for him.

The light was low, probably deliberately. There was some fresh fruit on the floor in front of him. As Randolph watched, his giant hand reached out to pick up a chunk of something orange, possibly a melon. Damba peeled it and Randolph realised Constance was putting this body through its paces, learning how its fingers felt as well as popping a few calories in ahead of the upcoming challenges. The fruit was sweet in Damba's heavy mouth. Randolph felt the odd sensation of jaw muscles he had never had before.

*We're in the enclosure in the building next door to the hotel,* Constance replied. *It's made from toughened glass, and if we can get out of it then exiting the building should be straightforward.*

*So how do we get out of the enclosure?*

*There's a double door entry, like an airlock. We get inside the first door, then we can use an access code to get out of the second one. It's designed so that personnel can get out in a hurry if they need to, but there's never a risk of Damba seeing the access code, because it's always entered when the first door is closed.*

*Do you think he would have learned it if he had seen it?*

*It's highly likely. He's a smart boy.*

Randolph watched as Constance took a few more moments to eat the rest of the fruit and walked slowly up to the glass at the front of the enclosure. Randolph had ridden in animals before, but never with this kind of clarity. Using animals as hosts was liking taking hallucinogenic drugs, a rush of incomprehensible sensations but this... There was a clarity here. The Symbio port made sense of neurological data that should have baffled and overwhelmed him.

The glass at the edge of the enclosure was semi-opaque, but by pressing up against it, he could see into the room beyond. It contained a table and some chairs along with a counter and some drawer units that looked like a food preparation area. There were no people in there.

*Seems like a good time to try* he said to Constance.

*Yep.*

Randolph was becoming more comfortable as a passenger. He was happy to consider them as a unit. They went over to the door, lifted a small cover and pressed a button. The door opened and they stepped through, a light coming on as they did so. The door closed behind them. There was another cover that opened to reveal a number pad. They stabbed in a code *6-7-1-4-8* and the outer door swooshed open.

*We need to get to the covered walkway between the hotel and the park behind it,* typed Randolph. *I have a colleague who will be there to collect us within two minutes of us appearing.*

*We're not going to meet your friend. Damba is not going anywhere. We need to get to the master control device from Krish's room.*

*So, we'll roam the corridors of the hotel, break into the room, find the device and sneak out again?* he typed.

*Yes, that's just what we'll do.*

*We're a 400 pound gorilla, in case you haven't noticed.*

*Yes. It sounds like a problem until you realise we're a 400 pound gorilla. No one's going to stop us.*

She had a point. Randolph stayed quiet so that Constance could get on with the task in hand. They went to the hotel room's door and rattled the handle. It was locked.

*Oh, I can help here.* Randolph was happy to play a part at last. *We need to look through those drawers for something I can use to pick the lock.*

*Or we could just do this.*

Their massive hand pulled the handle, which came away with ease. The door was still locked though. They raised a foot instead, leaning back into a powerful kick which smashed the door clean off its hinges and slammed it out into a corridor. Randolph expected people to come running, but it remained quiet. They walked along the corridor and came to an external door. Randolph anticipated the smashing of this door too. Instead they reached down and pressed an access pad which swung the doors open. They were in an alleyway. The rear doors were just across the way.

*That leads to the kitchens. Go in there*, typed Randolph.

*People will see us*, Constance replied.

*They're going to see us anyway.*

There was a young man in grubby chef's whites lounging against a low wall outside, smoking a cigarette. His eyes widened as he spotted the gorilla knuckling towards him. He vaulted the low wall and ran away. They went inside. There was a busy, steam-filled kitchen area with numerous staff shouting back and forth from workstations at stoves and sinks. The smells were rich and unfamiliar to the senses of a gorilla. Randolph was intrigued to find that the scent of grilled meat held no appeal for him. In fact it filled him with a primal sense of revulsion.

"Fuck me, what's that?" shouted someone. The staff turned to look and several of them screamed.

*Walk on*, Randolph told her. *Own the space.*

They walked through, ignoring the noise, focusing on the other side where they could access the main part of the hotel.

"Hey, you can't come through here!" yelled a middle-aged woman wearing thick glasses. Randolph wondered if her sight was so bad she hadn't realised she was addressing a great ape.

They turned to her and shook their fists.

*Roar!* Randolph commanded and the Constance-controlled ape did just that.

It was an impressive sound to Randolph, and it had the desired effect on the kitchen staff. They all shrank back, visibly terrified. Randolph was thrilled to realise he recognised the accompanying scent. He could smell fear.

*Pull down that trolley*, Randolph said.

As they reached the kitchen's exit, they swung an arm across to a large cabinet piled high with plates and pans. They pulled it down behind them as they left, partially blocking the door. The smashing of crockery followed them up the corridor which changed under their bare feet from tiles to thick hotel carpet. They followed the corridor round a corner and came face to face with a man and a woman.

*What now?!* said Constance.

The man and woman stared. The great ape paused nervously.

"Superb costume!" said the man.

The woman tugged on his arm, her face rigid. That smell of fear wafted over. "I don't think it's a costume."

The man looked more carefully and came to the same conclusion. The two of them backed up against the wall, pressing themselves flat.

"Urrgh." Randolph felt their vocal equipment trying to shape a sound. Constance was trying to put the couple at ease, but whatever she'd attempted to say wasn't coming out right. They carried on down the corridor, leaving the couple behind.

*It could be useful to form sounds,* Constance said. *Communication might be crucial at some point.*

*If you say so.*

"Urg ee araa." They coughed lightly, reacting to the strange tickling. "Urf ee shadaars arf affengun."

*Nice work. What are we trying to say?*

*I was doing some Shakespeare. 'If we shadows have offended, think but this and all is mended'. It's from a Midsummer Night's Dream.*

*You want a gorilla to quote Shakespeare? I mean, it will present an arresting sight in its own way, but don't we want it to help us scare people into doing what we want? Try something like 'Give me the device, you motherfucking asshole'.*

*Gorillas are peaceable creatures. We could cause Damba a lot of stress if we use intimidation too freely. How would you feel if someone took over your body and committed a load of crimes while they were in it?*

Randolph could not stop himself imagining what it would be like if someone took over his body and used it in ways he did not approve of. He pictured himself punching a stranger in the street. That wasn't so bad. He pictured himself punching a nun. That sounded almost comical if he'd heard it on the news, or if it happened to someone else; then he imagined actually being the one who did it and living with the consequences. He felt nauseous. Then he imagined punching a child, at which point he had to force himself to pull his mind back to the real world.

*Fine. Yes, you're right. Fuck me, I can't believe I'm saying this, but we need to think about the impact of our actions on Damba.*

*Yes, we do. Violence is a last resort and we should not instigate it if there's another way.*

They found the stairwell and climbed up to the fifth floor

without meeting anyone else. They went down onto all fours and ran along the corridor to the far end.

*We can cover ground more quickly like this,* Constance said.

*It feels good.*

They stood outside the hotel room door. Damba gently rapped on the door with fat knuckles.

*What are you doing?* said Randolph.

*Seeing if anyone's there,* she replied.

*Kick it in, Constance!*

Nobody answered, so they kicked the door in. It was a neatly-controlled kick, Randolph thought. It didn't smash the door or break it off its hinges, which might have attracted attention, so they were able to gently push it shut.

Randolph watched as Constance opened all of the drawers and cupboards and went through the contents. Krish hadn't brought loads of clothes and possessions, so it didn't take long to go through them. There was a safe inside the wardrobe, but it was open and empty.

*Right, I've searched all the obvious places. Are there any secret spy places that I might not have thought of?*

*Secret spy places?*

*Places Krish could have hidden it. Like in the toilet cistern.*

*Why in hell would your sales guy have hidden a valuable device in the toilet cistern?*

Constance insisted on looking anyway. They lifted the cistern lid and found only limescale. They upended the bed, even poking a hole through the fabric to check the void in the base, but it was empty.

*If it's not here then he's got it, hasn't he?* said Randolph.

*The Granada Mall,* said Constance.

*Oh, this gorilla's going on a road trip now, huh?*

*We've got to get the device. They could find out Damba's gone at any time.*

*Yeah, but I mean, seriously. A gorilla in a mall restaurant? That's going to draw some attention.*

They walked back over to the wardrobe and opened it up.

*Krish has quite a heavy build,* said Constance.

*You are kidding? You think we can pop a few items of clothing onto a gorilla and just walk into a restaurant?*

*That is exactly what I'm thinking.*

*You're mad if you think it will work. We need to go rescue our physical bodies and run for it.*

*We at least need to try.*

*Forget the Symbio port thing. Let's rescue ourselves and escape. You can get another job somewhere else.*

*You forget who's steering this ape.*

*Fine. Let's see what we can do. We'll take a critical view before we go anywhere though, yeah?*

Randolph watched as they flicked through the clothes. They dismissed suits and anything with too much structure. They reached for a shelf and pulled a t-shirt out from a pile. Holding it up, Randolph saw it was a very large size, but would it fit a gorilla? They pulled it over their head, and there was a loud ripping noise. They wriggled to pull it down and inserted their arms. There were more ripping noises. They stepped over to look in a mirror. Even though Randolph knew he was in the body of a gorilla, it was shocking to see his reflection. They were enormous! Damba's huge flat face, so animalistic and yet so human. He had never considered it before but, apart from language and basic etiquette, this creature could be his brother. The t-shirt was ripped, but covered the main area of their chest. They went into the bathroom and found a hotel robe. It was the usual oversized fit and actually accommodated their enormous body without too much difficulty.

*Hey, this is coming together!* said Constance.

*Insanity*, Randolph commented.

The harsh light of the bathroom made their face stand out against the white of the robe. They pulled the robe's hood over their head. It strained at all of the seams, but stayed in place.

*Need a pair of sunglasses,* Constance said.

*Because that 'gigantic heavyweight boxer trying to be inconspicuous look' needs to be rounded off with some sunglasses? We'll get some on the way. From somewhere.*

He realised with that last statement he'd given the thumbs-up to going ahead with this madness. He had been all for bailing from this mad mission. When it came to the money, he didn't really need it. When it came to his reputation, he could repair it soon enough. What he couldn't fix was the fact Constance was in charge and, painfully, morally right to boot.

Dressed, they headed out into the corridor. There was a yell.

There were cops in the corridor, two of them. They had their pistols drawn and aimed.

*Oh, I am so glad we hung around to get dressed*, said Randolph.

## 21

C onstance put her hands up.

*Are you seriously giving up?* said Randolph.

*They're cops! With guns!*

*You're an ape!*

She hesitated momentarily, then dropped to the floor as though dead, face angled towards the police officers.

*This isn't much better*, said Randolph. *Wait until they lower their weapons.*

*Already ahead of you...*

Out of her squinting eyes she saw the policemen really didn't know what to do. Why would they? They stood, fifty feet away, guns still pointed, but they were hardly going to shoot a comatose gorilla. They would probably do what any other underpaid public servant would do in similar circumstances – call in for instructions.

One tapped a comms button on his shoulder. The other, weapon also lowered, turned to confer with him.

*Now!* said Randolph, but Constance was already acting. She leapt up and ran for the nearest stairwell door.

Gorillas could handle stairs with ease and speed. Constance quite naturally leapt over the rail and swung down the final flight of stairs, consciously slowing to exit into the lobby. She made her way to the lobby and walked through with her head down and her hands in pockets.

*This isn't going to work*, said Randolph, despite the fact it evidently was.

She moved to a side exit. Damba was getting a number of peculiar stares, understandably. A hunched giant of a man wearing a hooded bathrobe was a peculiar sight. There were no frantic shouts of 'Gorilla!', which was better than could have been expected.

There were the sounds of an escalating commotion by the bank of lifts as Damba exited the building. Constance didn't look round and slipped out the side of the building.

*The Granada Mall is about two kilometres from here,* she said. *It's walkable.*

*The moment we are out of range from our ports, we'll be dumped back in our own bodies. We need to rescue ourselves first. Wave at that van!*

*What?*

She looked round. A plain white van was pulling over towards her. A skinny man leaned out of the window. His big thatch of wild hair brushed the top edge of the window frame.

*That man is called Spike,* said Randolph. *He is my assistant and he will help us. Give him a thumbs up!*

Constance did so.

"Glad I found you," said Spike. "Was wondering what the hell was going on. There are cops here, man."

The side door of the van slid open.

Constance shook her head. "Udda oo unkin'" she said.

"You've got to do something?" Spike asked.

Constance cheered at Spike's unaccountably accurate understanding. Probably the utterances of a gorilla were not that far removed from the underworld scum he associated with. She nodded.

"What's going on?" said Spike.

She waved for him to follow and hurried forward to the edge of the building. The van crawled after. The police van was still parked out front on the elegant driveway. There was one officer standing outside, seemingly chatting on comms. There was no sign of the others.

"Like I said, cops," said Spike.

Constance gestured to the van.

Spike's face fell. "Do not tell me you are inside that paddy wagon."

She gave him a sad nod and beckoned him to follow.

*What's the plan?* said Randolph.

*Ask the police officer to open it up.*

*Might work.*

Constance approached as circumspectly as she could, straight across the paved hotel forecourt. Spike's van was moving round on a service road which joined the driveway. Constance's plan, as limited as it was, relied on being able to approach the van without being seen. The police officer was thankfully too taken with the frantic chatter on his comms to notice the brute coming up behind him.

She leaned in and, as the officer began to turn, grabbed his right hand and hauled him up. The man screamed. This was less good but, on reflection, understandable.

She pointed firmly at the van doors and tried the handle. The police officer didn't seem to be picking up the signals and continued screaming. There were shouts and panicked noises from by the hotel.

"I think my furry friend needs to you open up," Spike called from his van.

The policeman was still not getting the message. It was surprising how long this guy could keep a scream going.

With a tut and a sigh, Spike got out of his vehicle stomped over, wrenched a key from the cop's belt and opened up the van. Constance could not help but be drawn to the sight of her own slumped body inside the rear compartment.

Spike took the police officer's gun and held it trained on him while Constance-(with Randolph)-in-Damba effected a rescue. She stepped in, snapped handcuffs and then, with one body held gently under each arm, removed them from the police van and transferred them to Spike's.

The suspension creaked as Damba climbed in. Constance looked back. Spike didn't know what to do with the police officer. The cop was a quivering mess on the floor.

Spike waggled the service issue pistol at him. "Go on! Run, mate! Run!"

The cop was too terrified to go anywhere. Spike dithered, lobbed the pistol into the nearest ornamental flower bed and ran back to his van. He ported directions to the vehicle before he'd even closed the door.

The gorilla team rolled over in the back (careful not to sit on the two humans) and patted Spike on the shoulder. Spike yelped, still fizzing with adrenaline.

"That was some crazy doo-doo, Randolph."

"An oo," Constance said.

"You're welcome. Now, what's next? Where you off to?" asked Spike.

*You can let me back into my own body now*, Randolph messaged.

*As if I trust you*, Constance replied. *I let you out and you have exactly what you want, a Symbio gorilla in the back of your van.*

*True*, he said. *But you also have me.*

And he was right.

Constance settled back on her haunches, drew Randolph's still body into her lap and cradled him, one hand circling his throat. From this perspective, it was surprising how fragile the human neck looked. It was just a sausage tube supported by bones.

*Very snappable*, she said, then released him back into his own body and his own sensory world.

She felt him jerk back to consciousness, automatically trying to pull out of her grasp. She held him tighter.

"Okay, okay," he squawked. "You got me."

Spike swivel in his front seat. "Right, boss—" He looked at Damba and frowned. "You got someone else in there?"

Randolph pointed at the body next to him. "Constance Wileman."

"Symbio?"

"She switched teams and..." Constance could feel a

weary sigh leave Randolph's body. "We've got to help her retrieve a master control device. In exchange for which she'll give us the port schematics."

"That's not what Mr Eight asked for."

"T'nod noitnem retsim et-ay," Randolph seethed in backslang.

"Oh, right."

"There's a place that serves alcohol at Granada."

The van immediately switched lanes. Spike tapped his skull. "Okay, we know the place."

Now stuck in a voiceless gorilla body, Constance felt out of the loop. She mimed writing with her free hand. Spike looked around and found a simple tablet for her.

She struggled to operate the basic interface with her large digits.

*Plans to get device?* she typed.

"This device, it would be some Symbio thing?" said Spike. "Obvious when we see it?"

*Maybe in briefcase*, she typed.

"Small enough to hide in a toilet cistern," said Randolph.

"What?" said Spike.

"Don't ask." He looked up at Damba's face. "You could leave this to Spike and me. We're resourceful guys."

*No way,* typed Constance and gave Randolph a meaningful squeeze.

"Okay, lady wookie. I get it. You have trust issues."

"Way I see it is you've got two options," said Spike. "You can either just burst in and shake them down. Or maybe we can sneak in the back and access the restaurant from the service side?"

*Yes.*

"So, any thoughts on a disguise that a gorilla can wear?" said Randolph.

"One that we can lay our hands on easily?" Spike blew out a long breath. "I got nothing right now. And I suspect a police-swarm will find us before long. This country might look like a tourist's playground, but the security services have this place sewed up tight. Here." He pointed as the van pulled off the highway into the parking lot of a western-style mall.

"Parking round the rear of the restaurant, right?" said Randolph.

"Indeedy-doo. I've actually got an idea."

"What?" said Randolph.

"Trust me."

*What?* Constance typed.

"Trust me, okay."

He hopped out of the vehicle and walked into the rear of the restaurant. Constance didn't trust him. She'd just met him, and he hung out with morality vacuums like Randolph Howard. She watched him until he was gone from sight. She grunted unhappily. What a day it had been. She was going to call the Alessa Survivors later and tell them how the big corporate meeting had gone. How was she going to spin this in a way that didn't look like a disaster?

*"Hi Helen. Yes, we had the meeting. We sold our souls to the evil corps and they want to create an army of soldier apes. Oh, yes, and I'm currently stuck in the body of a male gorilla with an international bodyhacker sat in my lap."*

"On the plus side," said Randolph unprompted, "you are

a very soft and warm cushion to lean against. Therapeutic almost."

Constance ran her fingers through the man's hair. It felt kind of appropriate in the moment.

"On the minus side," he continued, "your body stinks like a wet sheep rug and you've definitely got morning coffee breath. Minus the coffee."

The side door of the van slid open. Constance nearly snapped Randolph's neck in surprise. He coughed and retched.

"Right," said Spike. "The bad news is they're not buying my story about a speciality birthday greeting." He affected a snooty voice. "These have to be booked in advance and are only permitted in a private room, not the open restaurant." He gave a theatrical sigh. "I thought it was a stroke of genius myself. A gorillagram! Talk about hiding in plain sight!"

Constance nodded.

"So the good news is this." Spike produced a couple of kitchen aprons and a puffy chef's hat.

Constance made a questioning noise.

"I'm with the gorilla," said Randolph. "Say what?"

"You put those on and swagger through the place like you're a superstar chef on the way to do some important chefing." He held them up with a proud grin.

"What the fuck?" said Randolph.

"What?" Spike said. "You got this. It's all about attitude. Everyone knows that the front of house staff are the pretty ones and they keep the ugly folk back in the kitchen where they won't frighten the punters."

Constance wasn't sure this was a widely-held belief. She shook her head.

"You gotta trust me on this," said Spike. "You wear these things and swan through the place like you own it, a gorilla scowl will make you properly look the part. You might even get a Michelin star if you play your cards right."

She would have rolled her eyes but she hadn't mastered that level of body control.

"We could try it," said Randolph charitably.

Constance reached out a long arm, took the hat and jammed it onto her massive head.

Spike reached out. "Here, let me straighten that for you. Blimey, you look brilliant!" He stood back, grinning.

Constance thought Spike's enthusiasm was just a little too fervent. She reached for the pad and typed. *This is completely*

"—Stupid?" suggested Randolph. "Yes, but it might be all we have."

# 22

"I'll show you the way in," said Spike.

"You'd best stay here," said Randolph. "First sign of a police swarm or actual human cops, we need you to let us know."

Constance-in-Damba shuffled towards the door and stepped out onto hot asphalt. Randolph arranged the apron over her current outfit.

"My, you look divine, darling."

She gave his hand a warning squeeze.

"Hey. Ow, ow. Hey. Just trying to lighten the mood."

"Go through that far door and do a right," said Spike. "It will take you through the service door into the restaurant itself. Act superior and move quickly. You'll be fine. I'll wait out here for you."

They entered the restaurant. There was a hush from the diners as they walked in. They went with Spike's suggestion and scowled broadly at the crowd, while stalking boldly through the space.

Constance couldn't see her colleagues and the Manticore investors anywhere.

"Keep going. You're doing great," murmured Randolph. He threw a wave at some diners. "Showing the new chef around," he announced. "He's British. Swears all the time but his food's delicious."

The room was old-fashioned, with high ceilings. There was a central bar which formed a circle, capped by a high dome with a pineapple shaped top at its centre. It was kind of kitsch set in a modern shopping centre, but the kookiness didn't seem to affect the popularity of the place. Constance moved through and made menacing chef faces at anyone who glanced up. Remarkably, most of the diners looked away.

The scent coming to Constance's enhanced animal nose was not fear. It was more like ... something she might call social embarrassment. Were these people embarrassed at themselves for looking at a gorilla and thinking it looked like a gorilla? Maybe she'd unpack that later, but for now it was working as Spike had predicted.

"Twelve o'clock," said Randolph and nodded.

Krish, Martin, Dom, Don and Bozza were sat at a large corner table.

"Jesus hell," said Dom, liberally spilling his beer into Don's lap.

Krish looked up. His hand reached down his side towards a leather briefcase. "Okay, let's take this—"

Constance galloped forward, knocking chairs aside. She

grabbed the case with a wide swing of her powerful arms. Krish stood up, smiling nervously and edged around the table.

"Is this all part of the demo?" said Bozza.

"I don't know what's going on here," said Martin. He had his hands held out in a non-threatening gesture. "Hello Damba. We didn't expect to see you here."

"I have no idea who's taking a ride in you," said Krish. Constance saw he had the master control device in his hands. Furious, Constance ripped the briefcase open. A couple of pieces of paper fell out. The briefcase, symbol of office prestige rather than necessary equipment, was empty. In a less angry moment, Constance might have enjoyed the briefcase as metaphor for Krish's pathetic corporate soul, but now there was only anger and fear.

Krish activated the device.

A screaming ball of pain detonated in Constance's head. It felt like every synapse in her brain was being fired at some great and terrible distance and the core of her being was ripping into ragged chunks.

She screamed, first with Damba's own voice, then her own.

She jerked on the floor of the van, eyes wide.

The little guy, Spike, made a mewling peep of surprise. "Miss Wileman!" he said. "What's going on?"

## 23

Randolph saw Damba fling his massive arms up and scream. The roar which came out of that fanged mouth was both terrifying and terrified. Damba raised his fists and bared his teeth, and sprinted towards the bar.

"Constance!" Randolph called.

"Constance?" said Martin Drummond.

Damba scrambled up and onto the bar, but he didn't stop there. He hauled himself up on powerful arms and scaled the pineapple dome. Seconds later he was at the top, holding on with one hand and roaring at everyone in the restaurant. Most of the diners took this as the socially acceptable cue to scream and run for their lives.

Damba was driving his own body! Krish had ejected Constance.

"Seems our colleague has taken leave of her senses," said Krish.

The situation was unravelling fast. The ape was just there. The master control device was just there. If Randolph had time enough to find a quiet place and download fresh software to his wiped port he could hack Damba again and salvage something from the situation, but there was no time. This was a physical situation, and Randolph, despite his height and relative youth, didn't do physical situations so well. He was happy to throw other people's bodies into physical danger but respected his own too much to risk harm to himself.

"So, this gorilla is yours?" he said, adopting his best local accent. "I found her wandering along the highway."

Don was busy trying to mop beer from his crotch with a napkin. Dom was swearing and possibly doing a little praying.

Randolph tapped his lapel as though there was an ID badge there. "Ali Ababwa. Internal security. Is this your ape?"

Damba hammered the side of the dome and broke off a huge chunk of plaster. He hurled it across the room in rage. It landed on a large round table, sending food skidding across the table cloth and onto the floor.

"If I could just take a look at this..." Randolph reached forward to take the master control. A fat hand grabbed his wrist and bent it back.

"Hold your horses, mate," said Bozza. "Let's see some ID first."

"I have no idea what's going on, truly," said Martin.

"Let me deal with it," said Krish. He sat down and closed his eyes.

Restaurant staff were shouting and waving their hands.

The police would be on the scene shortly. Bozza's grip on Randolph was nearly as tight as the gorilla's had been.

On the dome, Damba huffed, sniffed and then slowly, calmly, climbed down. He stepped down onto the bar and then clumsily to the floor. He stopped to pick up a dropped plate and put in back on the nearest table.

"Krish?" said Martin.

"Oh, hell," Randolph whispered.

Sirens whooped as police vehicles poured into the mall parking lot. Constance edged to the van's open side door and looked out. A misty cloud of enhanced insects swarmed overhead. The eyes of local law enforcement were watching. Police jumped from their vehicles.

"We've got to get out of here," said Spike.

"We're not leaving him in there," said Constance.

She ran towards the cops and waved her arms. Running towards armed men was not something that came naturally to her, but she did it nonetheless. The police looked at her and she could see their gazes already sliding off her. Time to turn on the histrionics.

"It was huge!" she wailed. "A huge beast! It ran over there!" She pointed wildly at the main shopping mall building. "It was horrible!"

Several cops looked round. Some even started heading to

the mall proper. It almost certainly wasn't enough to throw them off the scent.

She reached out with her brain port, found Damba's port signal and jumped. Maybe the nearest cop would catch her lifeless body as it fell. Maybe it would help sell her weak girly plea for assistance. Or maybe she would come back to her body and find herself in handcuffs once more.

She was in Damba's head once more, now in a clutter of sensory feeds and protocols. She was riding along with someone else.

There was distant shouting from fleeing diners, but here, among the wreckage of the Symbio-Manticore celebratory beers, there was tense quiet. Big Bozza had Randolph pinned with his arm twisted behind his back. Martin, flustered, was apologising and trying to rationalise the situation on the fly. Krish sat in his seat, hand resting on the master control device, his eyes closed.

Ah. She was riding with Krish.

Krish had Damba standing still, squatting slightly, definitely doing his best to appear harmless and inoffensive. Constance could read interrogating data coming at Damba's brain port. Krish had detected her, maybe already working out who she was: returning to Damba after being forcefully ejected.

He opened a text window. *Have you gone mad? You've jeopardised the deal.*

She smiled inwardly. *I think we need to look at our security defences before we pitch to investors. Take a look at this, for example...*

Constance reached out and tried to remember what

she'd done in a state of near panic when Randolph had control of her body. It had seemed easy enough then, but could she consciously replicate and riff off it? She isolated the sensory and control data stream running from Krish to Damba. She grabbed, mirrored and reversed it.

She felt herself slump into Damba's body and assume control. Krish was gone. She turned her head to look at Krish. His eyes were open.

Krish blinked rapidly. He stared at his hands, amazed. He put a sleeve cuff to his mouth and nibbled experimentally at a button. He hooted in surprise.

"Krish?" said Martin.

Damba, now inside Krish, experimented with pounding his fists on the table and tugging at the tablecloth. He looked up at Constance, riding in his own body, and made an alarmed but intrigued face. He panted and gestured.

"What the hell?" said Dom.

Constance reached over and took the master control device from the table.

Krish jumped up onto the table. He stumbled on weak human legs, but rolled into a slightly awkward squatting position and picked up a bread roll.

"What is he doing?" said Don.

Constance turned and, with zero effort, separated Randolph from Bozza. She pushed Bozza forcefully into a booth seat and pulled Randolph towards the kitchens. She knew what she needed to find, and a walk-in larder was perfect.

"Are we hiding in here?" said Randolph.

She stopped him following her in, pressed the control

device into his hands and shut the door. It looked sturdy enough.

"I don't—" he began to say, his voice muffled, then perhaps he did understand. She heard him hurry off.

Constance sat on the floor, leaned against the wall and closed her eyes. She wished there was something she could say to Damba, a way to apologise, but after all the technology had allowed them, such communication was beyond her.

She cut the link and fell back into her own body.

R andolph sat in the van and scanned the parking lot. Spike had moved them some distance away, but the police were an uncomfortably constant presence.

"Too risky," said Spike, not for the first time.

"We wait," said Randolph.

"Maybe the police have taken her."

"Then we find out where they've taken her."

"You have the gizmo."

Randolph depressed the activation switch on the master control again, redundantly. "I sent the kill command. Damba's port is just grey goo trickling out of his ears now."

"A foolish move."

"The right one, I think."

There was a rap on the side window. The men turned, startled. Constance was looking at them. Spike opened the door and she climbed in.

"Not arrested," said Randolph. "Nice to see."

"The paramedics let me go when they saw there were richer people demanding their services."

"And now we leave, right?" said Spike. The vehicle moved under his silent command. "To an airport. In a neighbouring state. Maybe where we can get fresh IDs."

They passed a park resort van coming the other way, Constance turned to watch it.

"Damba will be fine," said Randolph.

"After all we've done to him?"

Up on the major highway, humming at speed into the west, it felt like they had left the fear and the cops behind them. Randolph knew it was an illusory feeling, but enjoyed it nonetheless. "Now, about those schematics..." he said.

"Did you just see the chaos?" said Constance. "And that was us trying to stop people abusing the power."

"I was going to say that maybe I should tell my client we were unsuccessful."

Spike laughed harshly. "Considering your debts to Mr Eight, you think that's wise?"

Randolph grunted at his colleague. "You will get into trouble for calling him that."

"You owe him over a hundred thou," said Spike. "But *I'll* get into trouble because I can't pronounce Papalapa-ding-dong-do..."

"Payapapa-Papala," said Constance. "The, er, octopus with human status in Greece?"

Randolph slapped Spike on the arm for blabbing.

"You owe money to an octopus?" said Constance.

"He's a very clever cephalopod," said Randolph.

"And Randolph is a very bad gambler," said Spike.

"Payapapa-Papala wants a brain port which allows humans to steer animals?" asked Constance.

"Communication is a two-way street," said Randolph. "Let's assume he's ahead of us all in recognising the potential."

Constance nodded, thoughtful. "Take me to him," she said eventually. "I think we need to talk."

# ABOUT THE AUTHORS

Heide Goody lives in North Warwickshire with her family and pets.

Iain Grant lives in South Birmingham with his family and pets.

They are both married, but not to each other.

# ALSO BY HEIDE GOODY AND IAIN GRANT

## Techin' Care of Business

**Buckle in for a high-tech ride through the corporate campus where things are about to go seriously off the rails.**

Gustav White loves working for Marlin. Marlin is the big tech company that everyone loves. You can buy anything from Marlin and next day delivery is guaranteed. They're even pioneering the next generation of self-driving cars and robot delivery drones. Gustav loves Marlin.

Ruby Jallow is an ethics consultant. She specialises in looking at Artificial Intelligence systems and solving the moral questions that arise. It's her job to make sure everything at Marlin is fair and honest and serves the general good. She likes her job.

Marlin was founded on the principle that it exists to serve everyone in the most efficient way possible. Marlin loves its employees and its customers.

Nothing bad will ever happen at Marlin. The self-driving cars won't start running people over. The delivery drones won't start violent turf wars with each other. Crash test dummies won't start questioning the purpose of their existence and seek out a more fulfilling life.

None of these things will EVER happen at Marlin. Marlin is good.

A prescient and satirical novel, perfect for fans of *The Circle*, *Severance* and *The Office*.

Techin' Care of Business

# Clovenhoof

Getting fired can ruin a day...

...especially when you were the Prince of Hell.

Will Satan survive in English suburbia?

Corporate life can be a soul draining experience, especially when the industry is Hell, and you're Lucifer. It isn't all torture and brimstone, though, for the Prince of Darkness, he's got an unhappy Board of Directors.

The numbers look bad.

They want him out.

Then came the corporate coup.

Banished to mortal earth as Jeremy Clovenhoof, Lucifer is going through a mid-immortality crisis of biblical proportion. Maybe if he just tries to blend in, it won't be so bad.

He's wrong.

If it isn't the murder, cannibalism, and armed robbery of everyday life in Birmingham, it's the fact that his heavy metal band isn't getting the respect it deserves, that's dampening his mood.

And the archangel Michael constantly snooping on him, doesn't help.

If you enjoy clever writing, then you'll adore this satirical tour de force, because a good laugh can make you have sympathy for the devil.

Get it now.

Clovenhoof

# Oddjobs

Unstoppable horrors from beyond are poised to invade and literally create Hell on Earth.

It's the end of the world as we know it, but someone still needs to do the paperwork.

Morag Murray works for the secret government organisation responsible for making sure the apocalypse goes as smoothly and as quietly as possible.

Trouble is, Morag's got a temper problem and, after angering the wrong alien god, she's been sent to another city where she won't cause so much trouble.

But Morag's got her work cut out for her. She has to deal with a man-eating starfish, solve a supernatural murder and, if she's got time, prevent her own inevitable death.

If you like The Laundry Files, The Chronicles of St Mary's or Men in Black, you'll love the Oddjobs series."If Jodi Taylor wrote a Laundry Files novel set it in Birmingham... A hilarious dose of bleak existential despair. With added tentacles! And bureaucracy!"
– Charles Stross, author of The Laundry Files series.

Oddjobs

Printed in Great Britain
by Amazon

34576707R00076